HELL ON EARTH

Sarah watched from the safety of the truck as a mass of refugees crawled, wrestled, and fought to capture a few beans, for every last granule of food. Others attacked the rebels, grabbing bags from them, ripping and shredding them. More beans, more fighting, screaming, and chaos. The rebels began beating people with their rifle butts and bandoliers. Shots were fired into the air to dispel the crowd, but nothing deterred them. There was food to be had, and it was clear from watching them struggle that food was the most important thing on earth.

Sarah had never thought of food and water in those terms; that in the end they were the only two things that mattered in life. These swarms of people would get to the beans or die trying. Watching them, Sarah knew that if they didn't eat something very soon most of them would not live out the week. That doctor—Nick Callahan—he hadn't exaggerated. He hadn't been grandstanding. This was hell on earth, and Sarah, holding a dying child in her arms, was right in the midst of it.

HELL ON EARTH

BEYOND BORDERS

A novel by **JAMES ELLISON**

Based on the screenplay written by **CASPIAN TREDWELL-OWEN**

POCKET STAR BOOKS
New York London Toronto Sydney Singapore

14017297

An *Original* Publication of POCKET BOOKS

A Pocket Star Book published by
POCKET BOOKS, a division of Simon & Schuster, Inc.
1230 Avenue of the Americas, New York, NY 10020

ISBN: 0-7434-6505-9

First Pocket Books printing October 2003

10 9 8 7 6 5 4 3 2 1

POCKET STAR BOOKS and colophon are registered trademarks of Simon & Schuster, Inc.

Manufactured in the United States of America

For information regarding special discounts for bulk purchases, please contact Simon & Schuster Special Sales at 1-800-456-6798 or business@simonandschuster.com.

PROLOGUE

*E*arly dawn in London. The year is 1995. Sarah Bauford nee Jordan sits pensively at a grand piano playing the theme of "Dreaming" from Schumann's Scenes from Childhood. She is in her early thirties, and her face—a work of classical beauty: clear, translucent, and possessing the kind of defined features that age well—is charged with pain and the power of love. She plays softly, her mind far away, her fingers moving from memory, liquid and beautiful. Moonlight paints a white path across the woman bent low over the piano. She is wearing a white bathrobe and her brown hair falls like a curtain over her as she plays and remembers.

Nick Callahan fills the landscape of her mind. She hears his husky voice, so full of passion and anger and rough humor, and the utmost certitude. She sees his dark hazel eyes, feels their heat like a wound deep inside her. She studies her fingers as they move and thinks, I still see you, all the times you never saw me. The times I was invisible to you. And though you may not know it yet, you are in me, you are a part of me forever. I will never let you go. Every syllable, every gesture and mood—even the blackest of your moods—your infectious faith, your incredible courage . . . all of it is memorized, imprinted on my soul.

How did I get here, you in another godforsaken country and me wanting to find you again; the truth is, from the first time I saw you, I never really knew how it would end. In fact, the only thing I am sure of is how it began. That night, so many years ago, you came in like a storm, it was all meant to be so civilized.

She had learned recently that Nick was working somewhere in the Caucasus. She imagined mountains, snowfields, endless vistas. She saw in her mind's eye great white-peaked ridges that dominated the barren plains stretched beneath from horizon to horizon. A world of vast mystery—mystery, danger, and fragile hope. Nick's kind of world.

She had inquired casually, not wanting to appear too inquisitive, about his welfare and his mission. She learned nothing beyond the obvious: He was in the Caucasus to make a difference. Nick's life was devoted to making a difference. And she was terrified that one day he would overreach his lofty goals and die. His desire to change the world, to bring hope to the hopeless, had led him to some of the most inhospitable and desperate places on earth.

One day your luck may run out, *she thinks.* There are some that say you are more rumor than reality. There are some that say you no longer exist except as a symbol of the struggle to defeat death. They say you finally ventured into the world's most inhabitable place—into that white wasteland.

The Schumann piece is coming to a conclusion, calling for a crescendo, but her playing remains muted, pianissimo. There is no life, only memory and yearning. She plays as though in a dream.

"So tell me," she whispers, eyes closed, feeling a wall of heat rise behind them, "in the end what choice do I have except to bring you back? If you're lost I have to save you." She fights the flood behind her eyes threatening to overwhelm her. "Whatever it takes, I will bring you back . . . just one more time."

The moon departs from the window. The sun is rising, beginning to bathe the room in a pale golden glow.

The day stretches ahead endlessly. Sarah trudges through it, memories of Nick pulsing inside of her. She wonders what she can do, knowing that she must do something to preserve her sanity.

Somewhere in the house, a phone rings.

PART
1

1

In 1984, Sarah Jordan was twenty-three and at the peak of her extraordinary beauty. She had never lacked for beaux, but had dropped them one after another when they turned serious, or as she called it, "clingy." She was too excited by life, to living fully the adventure of each day, to think of settling down. She stayed out late, partying with friends, and rose early each morning, believing firmly in the theory that "I'll have plenty of time to sleep when I'm dead." When she moved to London, where she planned to spend a year before returning to San Francisco and deciding on a career, she made a multitude of new friends and was captivated by the many accents and the subtle social nuances she was introduced to. The food is boring, she wrote home, but the culture is delightful.

Six months into her London stay she met Henry Bauford at an art gallery. Not long after, he invited her to a dinner dance held for a charity benefit run by his father. Henry asked her to dance and remained at a polite distance from her, their bodies never touching. He kept mumbling apologies. "I'm rather poor at this, I'm afraid. All my dancing sessions were wasted on me."

"I think you're a lovely dancer," Sarah told him, and she meant it. His movements were simple and straightforward (very much like his personality, as she was to learn later), and he possessed a kind of loose grace. His touch on her back as he guided her was light and feathery. When he thanked her and walked away—and had not returned by the end of the evening—she sought him out. He seemed somewhat surprised and flustered, and yet she could sense that he was pleased.

"You must be a masochist," he said as they danced the last dance together. "Do you enjoy having your feet stepped on?"

"Self-deprecating," she said with a smile. "I guess that makes you a proper English gentleman."

He blushed.

Two weekends later, he took her to Saturday dinner at Claridge's. They drank champagne, followed by a vintage Bordeaux with roast beef, and a Portuguese port with dessert. At first Henry was shy and lapsed into long silences, leaving Sarah to carry the conversational burden. But as he drank more, he grew loquacious. He had graduated from Oxford, had immediately gone to work for his father in the family-owned banking business, and had recently broken off an engagement. "She wanted to live in Johannesburg," he said with a slight turning down of his mouth, suggesting distaste. "Her family is there. Sorry. I wouldn't be caught dead in South Africa."

Henry was thirty-four, eleven years her senior, although he looked and acted much younger. There was a sweetness and a naïveté in his character that Sarah found appealing. He had a mop of unruly dark hair that flopped over his forehead and that he habitually shook away with an upward nod of his head—an endearingly boyish gesture. In fact Sarah found everything about Henry endearing: his mildly apologetic manner, a traditional behavior pattern in well-brought-up public school boys, the way his startlingly bright blue eyes danced with amusement at the least provocation, his slight stutter and blank look of bewilderment when he was embarrassed, either for himself or another.

By the standards of the Bauford family theirs was a whirlwind romance. They flew to San Francisco so that Henry could meet Sarah's parents, and three months later they were married in the Bauford's Anglican church. Their first few weeks as man and wife were idyllic—partying with friends, dinners, club hopping, play going. And most exciting of all was the lovemaking late at night. Neither of them was sexually experienced (Henry was a virgin till a good friend bought him an evening with a prostitute on his twenty-fifth birthday), but they were both experimental and willing to learn.

They were completely, rapturously in love.

Soon, though, Sarah began to chaff. Her life, she felt, was all dessert and no main course. Underneath her laid-back, happy exterior she was a serious young woman who was prepared to make demands on herself. She had been a first rate student; she possessed a keen mind and was determined to make a difference in the world—to find some way to help those less fortunate than she. She needed to do something vital with her life. She felt guilty rising each day at noon with a hangover and with the prospect of another day of idle pleasure stretching far into the night. Henry listened intently—or perhaps politely would be more accurate—but she sensed his indifference. She was beginning to accept that her husband, for all his charm and easy wit, was not an overly ambitious man. He loved his position in the world and his creature comforts. He was very much in love with her, for which she was grateful, but that was all that defined him. There had to be more.

They celebrated their first month of marriage with a group of friends. That night Sarah forced a conversation on Henry, who was drunk and dying to go to sleep. "I'm taking a job in an art gallery," she said. "I've put out feelers. With my background I'll have little trouble finding something."

"But why on earth do you want to do that, Sarah? God knows, we don't need the money."

"You work all day and I have nothing to do. That's not healthy."

"But your days seem so full," he protested.

"Full—I suppose that's true—but shallow. I go to lunches, shop, spend a lot of time on the phone, then wait for you to come home so we can have our nights out. That's not the way I want to live, Henry. I need more. I hope you understand."

He sulked, but knowing her husband, she knew that he would come around. A week later she took a job in a small gallery for little pay and long hours. But she was happy; her life now had some direction.

That winter, Lawrence Bauford, Henry's father, arranged for an elaborate Black and White Ball in an immense room at Claridge's Hotel. All the guests were to come dressed in black and white— no exceptions. The ball was to honor Aid Relief International: Healing Hands Across the World, 1964–1984, of which Lawrence was president. A wealthy, self-assured man in his late fifties, Lawrence Bauford was definitely old school, with his lockjaw, upper-class stutter and his Jermyn Street suits. He was also, unlike his son, extremely forceful, brooking no interference when he set out on a course of action. Where Henry had a habit of second-guessing himself, his father never doubted for a moment that his way was the right and only way. Sarah was drawn to his strength; he reminded her of her own father. She loved to listen to him talk about aid relief, about the complexities, headaches, and occasional successes, and she admired him for doing something worthwhile with his life beyond making money. Secretly she hoped that some of his grit and passion would rub off on Henry. She was beginning to realize that he needed to fill out more as a man, needed a little gravitas to complement his charm.

The night of the Ball was slushy and sleet-swept—London at its rawest. And the weather suited Sarah's mood. As she dressed carefully for the event, in a white gown with a black silk wrap and black Manolo Blahnik pumps, she concentrated her mind on her older sister Charlotte. She was going to see her that night for the first time in nearly a year. Thinking of her beloved Charlotte raised her spirits a little, but her mood remained somber. She had become restless again, not sleeping well and drinking far too much. She knew what the problem was; she needed to do something of more importance with her life. Her job in the gallery was not enough. There had to be a vital role for her to play in the world, and it occurred to her that she might have to go searching for it.

Her thoughts kept returning to Charlotte, as a protective measure against depression. The sisters often went long periods without seeing each other. As a reporter, Charlotte often took assignments outside of her Manhattan home; she always seemed on the go. Sarah had idolized her sister from childhood. Charlotte had fought her way up in her profession using wit and a keen investigative sense, letting nothing stand in her way. At the age of thirty she was well on her way to making a large career in TV news reporting. Sarah loved her for her ambition, but she also appreciated her sister's irreverence and ability to curse like a cab driver on a bad day. Charlotte had taught her little sister to drink and smoke and swear, and had also taught her to tell the truth, even if it hurt. "Once you start telling lies you have to remember them," she had said. "Now that's a pathetic way to clutter your mind." She also taught Sarah to stand up for herself, particularly with boys who were often deluded into thinking they were the sex that mattered. "Don't take any shit," she told Sarah, "from anyone."

Sarah put the finishing touches on her makeup and ran a testing finger over her carefully coiffed hair when Henry entered the room, tiptoed up to her, and put his arms around her waist.

"Ravishing," he said.

"Now don't smear my makeup."

"You're an éclair," he said. "A chocolate éclair —my very favorite kind. Shall I eat you?"

"Not now, Henry. We're late."

He regarded her closely. "You've been so serious lately. Not my laughing gal. Are you okay?"

"I'm fine. But you know how I hate being late."

He glanced at his watch. "We are running a bit behind. So—dessert later."

She smiled at him in the mirror and stuck out her tongue. "We'll see how good a boy you are tonight."

The ballroom was crowded by the time they arrived. They immediately gravitated to the dance floor and swirled around in a confined circle among the hip, the trendy, and the old money— all of those who gave large amounts to Lawrence Bauford's charity. Aid Relief International attracted a wide range of people, from sports figures, to film stars, to dowagers and landed gentry, to financiers and politicians, whether shady or not. The only common denominator was money. They were all here to be seen for having given generously, to be written about. Aid Relief International had suddenly become the hot charity, some twenty years after its founding, and everyone who was anyone wanted to be a part of it. The price of admission was strong support of the cause.

Sarah spotted her sister over Henry's shoulder.

Charlotte was unbuttoning her trench coat and making her way past a table of displays, brochures, and poster boards showing tastefully muted images of ethnic patients and attentive field doctors. Sarah whispered, "She's here!" in Henry's ear and broke away. She rushed across the crowded dance floor, Henry close behind her.

"Charlie!" she shouted, her favorite name for her sister.

Charlotte hurried to her, arms outstretched. "Sarah, my God, it's *you*."

They embraced. Henry stood apart from them, smiling awkwardly. He cleared his throat but said nothing.

"You're soaked," Sarah said, holding Charlotte at arm's length, inspecting her with a serious squint. "Drenched."

Charlotte pulled her close and whispered in her ear, "The fucking plane was late landing at Heathrow and there wasn't a cab to be had. I stood in the rain for nearly an hour."

"Poor Charlie."

"God's punishment. He always finds a way to get back at *moi*."

"You don't believe in God."

"Who's this good-looking guy standing next to you? Can it be Henry?"

Having forgotten her husband in the excitement of greeting Charlotte, Sarah whirled around and grasped Henry's arm.

"Darling, this is my sister Charlotte."

"So I gathered. Otherwise I'd say I'm in trouble."

"Don't be funny," Sarah said as her sister laughed.

"I'm Henry," he said. "So good to meet you." He extended a hand, which Charlotte took in mock gravity.

She turned to Sarah, an eyebrow lifted, wearing a devilish grin. "You didn't tell me he's gorgeous."

Sarah tilted her head and stared at her husband. "He is, isn't he?"

"More than you deserve, sis."

"Not true!"

Charlotte turned back to Henry, whose head was bowed as though he was trying to disappear.

"Did my sister tell you that insanity runs in our family?"

"Charlie!"

"Only kidding, Henry. You *did* know I was kidding, right?"

He managed a faint smile. "I rather thought so."

Charlotte leaned forward and kissed him lightly on the lips. He stood perfectly still as though frozen to the spot.

"I'm glad we're finally meeting. I've heard enough about you to fill a book. More specifically, a romance novel."

"Good things, I hope."

"Terrible things," she said, laughing. "Not repeatable. I'm so sorry I didn't make the wedding."

"No . . . no . . . It's quite all right."

Charlotte flashed a grin at her sister. "I'm not sure she's told you. I'm crap at appointments, simply the worst. I'm the victim of a work schedule you wouldn't believe. Here one minute, gone the next."

"Well . . . I actually . . ." Henry seemed to search for the right word without success. Not finding it, he shrugged and his shoulders slumped a little more.

"I may be unreliable," Charlotte continued, "but your wife is nuts. You do know that, don't you?"

"Nuts?"

"Let me explain. She believes that trees and flowers—all green things—have feelings. Roses can laugh, scream, cry. That sort of thing."

"Well, actually . . . I'm not aware . . ."

"Charlie, you quit picking on my sweetie *right now.*"

Ignoring her, Charlotte said, "I may be chronically irresponsible, but Sarah here is certifiable. So what's to choose?"

Henry smiled, glancing nervously at Sarah. "You're having me on."

"Having you on? I *love* that. Would you say it again?"

"I don't care that you are, actually. You're quite funny."

"And you're a good sport, Henry. I think we're going to be friends."

Henry extended an arm, which Charlotte promptly hooked hers through, as he said, "I would like you to meet my parents." At the head table sat Lawrence Bauford and his wife Lillias, where they were holding court. Mrs. Bauford was in her mid-fifties. She wore her hair in a severe no-nonsense bun and a spot of rouge, about the size of a thumbprint, on each pale cheek. Her black dress was closely tailored and worn precisely knee-length. Later Charlotte told Sarah that her mother-in-law looked exactly like Mary Poppins in one of her stricter phases.

Lillias Bauford was deep in conversation with a portly politician. The subject was pesticide control in tropical climates. Henry coughed politely, waiting for his parents' attention.

"Mum, Dad, may I introduce Sarah's sister Charlotte. She just now flew in from New York City."

Mrs. Bauford extended a hand and her features broke into a warm smile, removing a good ten years from her age. "How do you do?"

"My parents," Henry mumbled to Charlotte. "Lawrence and Lillias Bauford."

"You share the same surname," Charlotte said brightly. "How delightful. Everyone I know in the States is divorced—at least once."

Bauford stared at her blankly, then burst into laughter. "How amusing. You're having us on."

"Your son just used the same expression."

"It's British, dear," Mrs. Bauford said.

"Well, it's a pleasure to meet you, Charlotte," Bauford said. "I see that you've inherited the same beauty genes as my daughter-in-law."

"You're going to make me blush," Charlotte said, not blushing.

"Do you prefer to be called Charlie? I understand that's what Sarah calls you."

"Either will do, Mr. Bauford, or any other name you fancy. Right now I'd call me wet. Completely drenched."

"Come on," Sarah said. "I'll take you to the bathroom." She adjusted a lock of Henry's hair, which had fallen over his eyes, smiling fondly at him. "Be back in a sec'."

As Sarah led Charlotte across the crowded room, she exchanged smiles and greetings with many of the Baufords' intimates whom she had met in recent months. They passed close to the raised stage where a stand-up comic was in the middle of a monologue and paused for a minute to listen. The comic was dressed in a Sherlock Holmes–style hunting jacket, striped pants, white sneakers, and a beret. The total look was hilarious, adding immeasurably to his monologue.

"All anyone is talking about, friends, is famine this, famine that, famine the other thing. Famine,

famine, famine. Well, friends and fellow travelers, I have the perfect solution. No, really. I've solved the problem of world poverty." He paused for effect, then said: "Luggage. Big bloody traveler bags." He stared at the audience, wide-eyed. "And what's that one the gorilla used to jump on? What's it called?"

Someone in the audience cried out, "Samsonite."

"Yes, yes, that's right. Samsonite. That's it. Get yourself some *serious* luggage."

There was a smattering of laughter from the audience as the sisters moved on.

"Is that an example of British humor?" Charlotte asked.

"I guess so."

"I didn't understand a thing the man was saying. Did you? I mean it made no *sense.*"

"I just pretend," Sarah said.

The moment they stepped into the ladies' room they gave each other a huge uninhibited hug, squealing with delight at the joy of seeing each other. Their parents had divorced when Charlotte was fourteen and Sarah was eight, and the two girls, always close, had grown even closer. They needed each other for comfort. There had been the bad times when they had felt as though it was the two of them against the world. When, two years after the divorce, their parents had tried to separate them—Sarah staying with her mother in San Francisco and Charlotte moving down to Santa Barbara with her father— Charlotte had put her foot down. She was sixteen by then and very grown-up, a senior in high school, extremely outspoken and headstrong. She said in no uncertain terms that the sisters would stay together. Mrs. Jordan gave in immediately—her older child had always cowed her— but when Mr. Jordan balked, Charlotte threatened to run away with Sarah to New York City. She had two thousand dollars in her bank account, saved from baby-sitting, and Mr. Jordan knew her well enough to know that she was dead serious. Finally he capitulated.

Charlotte studied Sarah closely. "Just get a load of you, li'l sis. You look fabulous."

"So do you, Charlie."

Charlotte lit a cigarette, let it droop from a corner of her mouth and grinned. "Bull*shit*. I look like Ivana Trump after she went a couple of rounds with The Donald."

"You just need a little tweaking. Come here."

Sarah drew Charlotte over to the mirror, removed a brush from her purse, and began working on her hair.

"It's a lost cause," Charlotte said as she sent up clouds of smoke. "Give it up. Love me like I am."

"Just be quiet and hold still." She applied eyeliner and lipstick. "I'm going to make you into the raving beauty you actually are."

"Lots of luck. Remember—you've got mother's touch of violet in your eyes. I don't."

"But you have father's beautiful dark eyebrows. We're even."

As Sarah worked, the tip of her tongue protruded from the corner of her mouth—a habit she had when concentrating.

"So . . . what do you think of him? And I want an honest answer. No funny jokes, please. Or the usual Charlie sarcasm."

"I think he's a sweetheart, if you can stand the brutal truth. Mind you, I'm basing this on precisely 22.4 seconds of acquaintance."

"I thought that's what journalists and reporters do."

Charlotte gave Sarah a playful shove. "Hey, *you* should talk. You married the guy after only three months."

"So what?" Sarah said, laughing. "I love him. It took me about 22.4 seconds to figure that out."

"It wasn't a shotgun wedding, was it?"

"Shut up, Charlie."

"I'm just asking. I hope you checked his résumé."

"I certainly did not, but I'll bet you did."

"Are you accusing your older sister of being overly protective?"

"I guess you could say that."

Charlotte hesitated for a moment, then said: "He's very gentle. You can tell he has a kind soul.

And yes—he's drop-dead gorgeous. Your classic hunk, British division."

"He is, he *is,*" Sarah said, her voice rising with excitement. "And sexy and fun. And wild, too. He just needs a little prodding because it's all been bottled up in him."

"And so veddy, veddy English. You married a really English Englishman."

Sarah put her hands on her sister's shoulders and drew her close. She stared into her eyes. "Remember what we used to say to each other when we were kids—'Liar, liar, pants on fire?'"

"I remember."

"And we always said we would never lie to each other . . ."

"And we haven't."

"Charlie—look into my eyes. Do you have any doubts about us—about Henry and me? You are the one person on earth I trust."

Charlotte returned her intent stare; neither blinked nor looked away. They communicated to each other from deep within themselves. She said finally, "I'm surprised, but not displeased."

"What do you mean? Explain."

"I guess I always thought you'd marry a man like Daddy. The masculine, driven 'can-do' type. You have a lot of Mother in you, and I figured you'd need that." Charlotte shrugged. "I was wrong."

"But I'm not Mother."

"No, you're not."

"I have some of Daddy in me."

"You do."

"Charlie—do you really like Henry? It's so important to me that you do."

Charlotte leaned forward and kissed Sarah's cheek. "I really, really like him. He just reeks of decency. The looks are just a lucky bonus."

The sisters embraced again; something important had passed between them and been settled.

"How are things at home?" Sarah said.

"Home?" Charlotte looked blank. "I thought this was your home now."

"*Very* funny."

"Home's fine. I call Daddy and Mother once a week. That's obligatory. And I'm looking for a larger apartment. You have to be rich to live in Manhattan. If I found a halfway presentable man with the right apartment, I'd marry him in a heartbeat."

"*Very* funny. And how's work?"

"Same old, same old. Dull some days, exciting once in a while. But I'm getting antsy. There are great stories for me out there. Last week I covered a ten-car pileup on Fifty-fourth Street. I did have a minute with the mayor last month. A high point. I had the awful feeling he wanted to pinch me."

"But things are looking up, right?"

"Sure," Charlotte said, one eyebrow arched. "Top of the news pile, honey. Your big sis is wowing them."

"You will, you know, Charlie. One day you'll be top dog."

Charlotte grinned. "Well, I like the top part anyway."

Once Sarah finished fussing with Charlotte, her older sister spun around to the mirror.

"My God, girl, what are you doing to me? I'm tarted up like some damn hooker."

Sarah thumbed her nose at her, a throwback to their childhood. "Don't be an ass. You look fantastic."

Slowly their smiles faded. They regarded each other eye to eye, really looking, drinking each other in.

"Hey, it's good to see you, little sis. I missed you like crazy. We can't go a year again."

Sarah reached for her hand and said, "We can never go a year again." She cocked her head, studying her sister. "Wait—you know you're right. You *are* a hooker. I can't have you scandalizing the Baufords." Grinning, she removed some of Charlotte's makeup.

When they returned to the ballroom, a lugubrious Oxbridge type, Philip Outerbridge, solemnly in love with the sound of his own voice, was holding forth at the head table. Mrs. Bauford seemed riveted to his words.

What an actress, Charlotte thought. She knows how to play these rich and powerful men like a master conductor.

And Sarah was thinking that her husband looked quite beautiful, almost like a woman.

Outerbridge said, "Now the fact of the matter is, you take any third world country, doesn't matter which one. The problem, you see, isn't industrial infrastructure or religious extremism or even Communism—it's the vagina." He grinned at the ladies, his eyes lost in pale folds of fat. "Yes—the vagina, I'm afraid. That much the Muslims have worked out."

Bauford, puffing thoughtfully on a cigar, turned to his wife and said, "Lillias, did you hear that? Apparently your genitals are responsible for world suffering."

Mrs. Bauford slipped a cigarette between her lips as she said, with just the hint of a smile, "Perhaps I need a government health warning. I could stick it on my knickers."

A burst of laughter rose from the table, which she was canny enough not to join. She remained deadpan.

God, that woman is *good*, Charlotte thought. And very, very clever. Never underestimate these middle-aged rich ladies. They can eat you for lunch.

Poor Henry, Sarah thought. He spends way too much time listening to this silly prattle. He really needs something more in his life.

As Philip Outerbridge droned on, the stand-up comic was heating up.

"Let's return to that luggage for a moment. We all love to obsess on luggage, don't we? Find it, buy it, steal it—just make sure you *have* it." He reached down, pantomiming grabbing a handful of dirt. "This is why. All around you is dirt. You can't eat it, you can't drink it. Dirt won't rescue you from the hell of poverty. What you have to do, friends, is get away from it—far, far away. So pack your bags and get the hell out. *Leave! Now!*"

The audience laughed appreciatively; the comedian had found his stride now and was working the crowd smoothly. There was one man, however, who did not join in the general merriment. He stood apart, in an island of isolation, his hands clasped behind his back and his trench coat open to reveal a black shirt and a solid gray tie. He ignored the comedian and was staring intently at the Bauford table. After a moment he squeezed his Asian girlfriend's hand. "I'll be back in a minute," he said, his voice surprisingly soft in such a dark and hooded countenance. "Wait for me right here."

He headed for Lawrence Bauford, careful to touch no one as he moved between the tables and around people milling about. Seeing him coming, Bauford rose, excused himself and slipped away from his group. The two men shook hands, neither of them smiling, and moved away from the table.

"Larry," the man said, grasping Bauford's hand

uncomfortably hard. "Good to see you again, old man."

Bauford regarded the man with a slightly raised eyebrow. Meticulously polite and yet lowering the temperature a little as he bit off the words, he said, "Forgive me, Mr. Steiger. I'd have popped over earlier, only I didn't know you were invited."

"I was in town, so I thought I'd drop in. I hope you don't mind."

"Not at all. Of course. More than welcome."

Bauford's gaze slid for an instant to the beautiful Asian girl.

"I met her in Phnom Penh," Steiger said softly, nudging Bauford's arm. The older man stiffened and leaned away. "No family," Steiger continued, running a finger quickly across his throat. "Dead."

Bauford nodded, clicking his tongue. "Ah. A pity. These things are such a shame, aren't they?" He hesitated, then added, "And what were you doing there?"

"What was I doing?" Steiger said with a thin smile. "What does anyone do there?"

"In your case, I'm not certain, Mr. Steiger. Perhaps you could enlighten me."

"'In your case,'" Steiger repeated. "I'm not sure how to take that, Larry."

"Take it any way you wish."

Steiger's small black eyes stared into Bauford's until the older man looked away. "I heard a rumor that Aid Relief International is withdrawing from Ethiopia."

"Oh?"

"Is there any truth in it?"

"You yourself just called it a rumor."

"You're being evasive," Steiger said. "If it's true it strikes me as very strange. I mean, where is your work needed more than in Ethiopia? They say you came under pressure to pull out." Steiger watched the older man closely, the way you might study a poker player about to raise, fold, or stand pat in a crucial hand.

"And who might 'they' be?" Bauford finally said.

Steiger shrugged. "People."

"Well . . . some people might think that."

"Why?" Steiger said.

"Well, I'm afraid I must state the obvious. They might consider the fact that Ethiopia is a Communist regime and that Mrs. Thatcher considers Communists to be fractionally more advanced than the amoeba."

Steiger's lips compressed into a thin line and his small eyes grew smaller.

"So the people starve because some pretentious little African believes in Marx. Is this what you're telling me?"

"Please, Mr. Steiger. You know better. Mengistu and his cronies have just spent two million dollars celebrating the tenth anniversary of their rotten corrupt regime. As the kids say, what's wrong with that picture?"

"People are starving, Larry."

"The money's clearly there. Mengistu fiddles while Ethiopia burns."

"So you're out," Steiger said.

Bauford inclined his head slightly in silent assent.

"Pity," Steiger said. "I was going to be very vulgar and write you a check. But obviously there's no point in it now. If you're not in Ethiopia, you won't be in a position to assist my colleagues there."

Bauford flinched, then all emotion leeched from his eyes; they were gray and dead. "Good to see you, Mr. Steiger," he said, clearly not meaning it. He returned to his table, leaving the man staring at his back.

Once Bauford took his seat, Henry leaned close to Sarah and said, "Be back in a minute." He approached the stage, smiling and nodding at various friends. At the steps leading to the stage he drew a pretty, tangle-haired charity worker aside. "Okay, Beatrice," he whispered. She in turn signaled the comedian, who quickly brought his act to a close. She took the mike and said, "A round of applause, please, for Maurice Ruggles." She clapped and many in the audience, mainly the younger members, joined her.

"And now, everybody, I would like to introduce

Mr. Bauford's son Henry, who has an announcement to make. Henry?"

He stepped on stage and accepted the microphone from Beatrice. He cleared his throat a number of times and stared out at the audience with a shy smile. "If you hear a strange sound in the room," he began, "it's my knees knocking."

This drew applause and laughter. Henry's charm immediately won them over.

"Ladies and gentlemen, as you know, we're here tonight to show our appreciation to Lawrence Bauford for all the great work he's done as chairman of Aid Relief International and to honor the charity's progress over a generation. Those of you familiar with my father know him as a man of few words, and always to the point. I should say *quite* to the point." Henry accepted the laugher with a gracious nod. "So, out of respect of his verbal economy, I will simply ask you to raise your glasses and toast . . . Lawrence Bauford."

The room rose and gave a loud toast, with many a "Hear! Hear!"

When the room grew silent, Henry looked at his table, smiling at Sarah and giving her a slight wave. "Oh—and Lawrence Bauford's daughter-in-law of these past three blissful months—my wife Sarah." He gestured to the side of the stage. "Can we get on the first table please?"

A spotlight swept the floor, finally finding Sarah. Playfully, she stuck her tongue out but she looked more embarrassed than happy. Charlotte waved at Henry, grinning devilishly. The elder Baufords did not look amused.

"Ladies and gentlemen," Henry continued, "I give you my wife—metaphorically, of course . . . And it still amazes me to say it—Mrs. Sarah Bauford."

Roars of good-natured cheers and applause filled the room. Pinned in place by the spotlight, Sarah stood very still, hands close to her sides. She hated every second of this grandstanding but forced herself to smile for Henry's sake.

Suddenly a burst of angry voices tore through the room, changing the mood from lighthearted to apprehensive in just seconds. Some sort of commotion was taking place at the entrance, and many in the audience stood to get a better view. Henry, still standing on stage, was drowned out and forgotten. Someone at the door shouted, "Who are you?" Another voice shouted, "Who let the cameras in here?"

People backed away en masse from the tables near the entrance. A striking man with blazing eyes barreled down the aisle toward the stage. He pulled a young, painfully thin African boy along by the hand, and they were followed closely by a phalanx of media. The room was in an uproar.

"Jesus," Charlotte said with a startled glance at Sarah. "Things are popping in staid old England."

She reached for her purse and pulled out a note-book and pen and began taking notes.

The man was suddenly standing at the Bauford table, giving Sarah a chance to take him in. He was large and deeply tanned, his intense expression strangely attractive. He cast that intense look at Lawrence Bauford, who was stunned and gray-faced by the sudden turn of events. The stranger grabbed a champagne bottle from the table and said, still staring hard at Bauford, "Thanks for the contribution. Every drop and morsel counts." The remark held a note of contempt, but the voice was melodious and deep. He turned his burning hazel eyes on Sarah, and for a split second he seemed about to say something, then turned away and leaped on stage.

Bauford turned to his security chief, Rolly Edwards, who had appeared at his side seemingly out of nowhere, and said quietly, "Get him out of here."

The stranger, still holding the young boy's hand, stood facing the audience, his legs spread wide apart in a fighting stance. Flashbulbs revealed that the boy, who wore a thick gray track-suit with a hood, was no more than ten or eleven. His face, although emaciated, was alert and curious; his large dark eyes took in everything in the room. There was a sharp whistle of feedback as the stranger grabbed the mike from Henry's hands. Henry started to protest but then backed away. The stranger swigged some champagne.

"What are you doing here?" Henry said. "What do you want? You have no right to barge in—"

"Back off," the man interrupted. "You've had your say. The floor's mine now." He held the champagne bottle by the neck like a club as he turned again to the audience. "Let me introduce myself. The name is Nick Callahan. I'm a doctor—a field doctor. I try to save lives. I don't always succeed. In fact I usually don't succeed. If you ask me, this event you're attending here, it's a bloody rip-off. A thousand quid for an overcooked meal and a dry hump on the dance floor. Not to mention the platitudes you'll hear from the folks in charge. But hey, we're all getting drunk for a good cause, right? Cheers!"

To a chorus of hisses and boos, Callahan raised the champagne bottle and emptied the contents at his feet, splashing some of it on his work boots.

"Twenty quid a head right there," he said. "Divvy up the room rental—maybe another twenty. Thirty on catering. Fifty quid on overhead—maybe that's conservative. Maybe it's a whole lot more. But who cares? It's only money. Money for this wonderful cause. Money so you can all feel good about yourselves." He turned to his young companion and said with a grin, "There you go, JoJo. That's your cut. The world is a really swell place, isn't it? All these people thinking about you as they stuff their faces and swill champagne."

He handed the champagne bottle to the young African, who stood there staring at the upturned bottle. He scanned the crowd of angry, confused, and bewildered faces, his own expression as confused and bewildered as theirs.

Callahan continued, his voice hard and fierce: "I'm sorry—I've neglected to introduce my friend. His name is JoJo. He is a ten-year-old African boy whose spirit and knowledge of the heart of man is ancient. He has not had a day of school in his life. He has never eaten the usual three meals a day. He has never had a roof over his head. He has starved most of his life and has been close to dying many times. Actually he is curious about your dinner. You see, when I found him he was so starved he was trying to eat his own tongue. Ever tried that? Funnily enough, they don't serve Caesar salad with that dish. No—I'll be honest—and I do so want to be honest—he was a pile of bones when I found him and lying in a pool of shit. And I don't mean civilized shit either. I mean this was the yellow stuff—liquid fucking evil."

Bauford was now standing beside his security chief, shaking with anger. "I said get him off, Rolly. What the hell is the problem?"

Edwards shook his head, looking grim. "We've got a sticky situation here, Mr. Bauford. I don't like it. There's media all over the place. You want me to storm the bloody stage? It won't look good in tomorrow's papers."

- 35 -

"For God's sake," Mrs. Bauford said, "do *something*. This is preposterous."

"We're doing what we can, ma'am."

"Henry looks absolutely ashen," she continued. "I wish he'd put this dreadful man in his place."

Charlotte, who had been unobtrusively scribbling in her notebook on her lap, looked up and whispered to Sarah, "This guy is totally out of his mind—some kind of raging Hamlet."

Sarah did not respond. Her eyes were fixed on the young African boy. He was beautiful and yet she could see death in his face. She caught a sob in her throat, powerless to look away, powerless to stop the darkness that had entered her soul. She was aware that she was feeling some of the man's anger, and her anger, like his, was directed at herself and the others in the room.

Callahan pulled JoJo close, in a protective embrace. He scanned the audience—pinned to their seats, outraged, yet thoroughly hypnotized by this spectacle that had been thrust on them seemingly out of nowhere.

"Here's what you need to know," Callahan went on. "My friend JoJo here is no special case, not by a long shot. I've got two thousand kids in my camp in Africa with the same problem—some even worse, if that's possible—and some asshole here just pulled my funding. So I guess we'll have to feed 'em flies. Now JoJo, he just doesn't understand why. He feels he has a right to know why.

He's crazy enough to consider himself a human being, no matter what the world thinks. So I showed him this . . ."

Callahan unfolded a letter and began to read. He read slowly, without inflection, emphasizing each word equally: *"Due to the repressive political climate, we can no longer sustain a relief presence in Communist-supported Ethiopia . . ."*

Bauford sat tight-lipped at his table. Callahan regarded him for a long moment. The room was suddenly silent. Finally Callahan said, "Maybe you can enlighten us, Larry. Is that a fair statement of how things stand? Or were you hoping for a more positive spin? Is it fair to say that you've given up on JoJo and the thousands and thousands like him?" Callahan did a flourishing wave with his right arm and a bow. "The floor's yours, Larry. Enlighten us."

"You've said your piece, Doctor Callahan. Now you can leave."

"Not quite yet. We're all still in a partying mood. How about your coming up here, Larry? Or is it Lawrence? Come on! The kid just wants to hear it in words he can understand. Two thousand lives, old boy. That's the math. What does that buy you? A new car? A new pair of tits for the wife?"

Bauford took a step toward the stage, raising his hand, palm outward, as though to stop traffic. "Really, Doctor Callahan, there is no need for this rant. You've had your say. You've managed to make a perfect ass of yourself. Now step down."

There were scattered boos in the back of the room, which Callahan acknowledged with a wave and a smile.

"You heard what my father said," Henry put in.

Callahan turned toward him with a quick angry swivel, staring him down. "You're deaf, aren't you? The golden sonny boy hasn't heard one fucking word I've said." He dismissed Henry with a shrug. He spotted security guards moving slowly toward the stage along the side walls. In the distance was the sound of an approaching siren.

"Come on, Larry," he said, speaking more quickly now. "Our time together is nearly up. Don't be shy. I've got a camp with thirty thousand people dying at the rate of forty a day. I've got measles, cholera, typhoid—every miserable fucking disease known to man. Six weeks from now, without any help, they'll all be dead. It may not mean jack shit to you, *but they are human beings.*" Callahan cupped his hand and wiggled his fingers, gesturing toward himself in a come-hither way. "Come on, man, *talk* to me."

A young man rose and hurled a banana toward the stage; it landed at Callahan's feet. For a moment his momentum was stopped and he seemed uncertain how to proceed.

The audience also seemed poised in a kind of limbo. Then an embarrassed titter built into loud laughter and a scattering of applause and whistles.

Callahan seized the moment. He bent over and picked up the banana and slowly began to peel it. The applause faded and a hush of anticipation fell over the audience. Handing the peeled banana to JoJo, he nodded his head. Shyly, tentatively, the boy ate the fruit. He ate it slowly, chewing each bite many times, never taking his eyes from the crowd.

Callahan waited until the boy had eaten the last bite and then said, "I get it. The old monkey joke—right? You want him to go 'oo oo,' just like a monkey. He'll go 'oo oo' for you, you can trust me on that. I mean, you just fed the boy a banana, a boy who has spent most of his short life starving. Hey, JoJo, go 'oo oo' for the folks in the audience."

The African boy blinked at Callahan, who thrust the microphone close to his face as he whispered something to him. The boy's sweet soft voice echoed around the room: "Oo oo. Oo oo. Oo oo . . ."

Now there was absolute silence. The humiliation of the moment was ricocheting, end to end. Sarah stared at the table, biting her lower lip and trying to shut out the angry thoughts. Charlotte continued to take notes beneath the table, hoping that she wasn't noticed.

Callahan let the silence grow to unbearable

lengths before saying, "There are three hundred calories in one banana. That's more than he gets in a day. Believe me, he'll do whatever you want. Want him to squeal like a pig? All you've got to do is ask."

The security guards converged on stage and Rolly Edwards stepped forward, his arm stretched toward Callahan in a pacifying gesture.

"Doctor Callahan, you must leave the stage. You must leave now."

"I don't think so," Callahan replied, putting a protective arm around JoJo.

Edwards, with a slight head gesture, moved forward and grasped Callahan's arm. As Callahan tried to shake him off, the other guards advanced. With a roar of rage Callahan broke free and swung at one of the guards, landing a glancing blow to the jaw that knocked him to his knees. As flashbulbs started going off like a light show, Callahan was tackled and thrown to the floor. JoJo was buried under two guards. Callahan struggled to reach JoJo. "For Christ's sake, *leave him alone.* Can't you see he's sick?"

Journalists and photographers were now on stage, hopping around frantically like kids at recess, lights popping, the whole room buzzing. Callahan fought off two guards and managed to get to his feet and pull JoJo free from a tangle of arms and legs. Four guards manhandled them toward the exit.

A number of journalists surrounded Bauford, who kept a nervous eye on Callahan and the boy.

"Mr. Bauford," said one elderly journalist, enunciating his words in classic BBC style, "do you have anything to say? Are you, in fact, pulling out of Ethiopia? As Callahan said, thousands of people are starving there. If the funds are available, how can you countenance a withdrawal at this point?"

"What country is in greater need of aid?" another reporter put in.

Bauford noticed Charlotte standing at the back of the crowd of reporters, notebook in hand. When he caught her eye, he frowned, eyebrows knitted together.

"Ethiopia is a paranoid Communist state," he said, his voice strained with repressed emotion. "Did Doctor Callahan tell you that? No. Of course not. Did he tell you that Mengistu appropriates all foreign aid for his own purposes? Of course he didn't. Did he tell you that the famine was caused by collectivization? But then why would he do that? If Callahan is not a Communist himself, he is certainly in sympathy with its cause."

"And yet, Mr. Bauford," the elderly journalist began, but Bauford spoke over him, saying, "One hundred thousand dead because of their insane policies—and that man has the gall to use a child as a prop. That is so bloody cheap. Doctor Callahan may be a good doctor, but he's a disgrace as a human being. I have nothing further to say."

At the curb outside the hotel, a driver opened the back door of a limousine for Sarah. Her face was set in a rigid frown as she watched two police cars turning out of the hotel's service alleyway, lights flashing. She caught a glimpse of Callahan in the back seat of the first car, flanked by two officers. In the second car was JoJo accompanied by a female police officer. Sarah looked away, dimly aware that Henry was saying something to her. She slipped into the car. The driver opened the other door for Henry, who got in beside her and took her hand. Charlotte stood beside the car, her hands deep in her trench coat pockets, watching people file by and listening to their comments. She was in a sour mood. Mrs. Bauford had scolded her for taking notes, telling her it was "not the thing to do." Rather than try to defend herself and give in to her notorious temper, Charlotte had stalked off without a word.

Henry brought Sarah's hand to his lips. "My darling . . . are you okay?"

"Not really. I think I'm in shock."

"I'm terribly sorry about what happened."

She turned to her husband, and there was a look in her eyes—a cool appraisal, a determination—that he had not seen before and was not sure that he liked.

"What *did* happen?" she asked. "It seems to me that so many things were going on."

He brought out his charming grin from his bag of facial tricks.

"The entire charade was uncalled for," he said. "There was simply no need for it. Callahan's spiel was nonsense. He was grandstanding, and it was vile the way he used that child."

"Do you think it was a charade, Henry? People are dying. It seems to me the doctor was trying to make a point. Maybe he didn't go about it the right way—"

"Just forget about it," Henry said, more sharply than he intended. "It's complicated. There are serious political issues involved."

"I think I'm capable of understanding them, you know."

"I'm sure you are." He paused briefly. "Charlotte annoyed my father by taking notes. Was that really necessary?"

"She is a reporter, Henry."

"But I consider this rather a family affair. I trust she isn't planning to run to her people with this."

"I have no idea what she plans to do," Sarah said. "And it's really not my affair. Or yours."

In their brief life together this was as close as they had come to a quarrel. They were both suddenly overwhelmed with guilt and remorse. Their plan was to create a perfect union, without ugliness or dissension, and suddenly they sensed a gulf, a little abyss, and neither of them wanted to look into it too closely.

"Listen, my dear Sarah, I'm sorry if I've been a bit short with you. This has been trying for us all, and I'm afraid the stress has gotten to me." He reached for the door handle. "I'll be home as soon as I can."

"Where are you going?"

"I should probably help Dad with the press. They're killing him in there. The last thing we needed was that ass of a doctor to muck things up."

Sarah felt a wave of fear pass through her, all the more profound because she did not understand its source.

"Don't go," she said. "Stay with me. I need you."

Henry grinned, happy to be restored to his position as the male in charge. "Charlotte will look after you."

He kissed her and hurried off. Her eyes followed him, filled with tears and a look of unbearable sadness. It was a look that he would never see.

Later that evening a police van came to a halt outside a brick building at Heathrow. Two police officers jumped out and met an immigration officer who signaled them to open the rear door. Six immigrants hopped down the steep step to the ground—a pair of glum Sikh Indians with dancing terrified eyes; three Bangladesh males in their thirties chattering at high volume; and JoJo, his head hunched deep inside his hood, trying to appear invisible. A seventh immigrant, an old Chinese man, refused to leave the van. He sat stiffly, with a look of fierce resolve, muttering to himself in Mandarin.

"Sir," said the immigration officer. "Please— you have to come out."

The old man looked at him blankly, continuing to mutter.

With a nod from the officer, the two policemen piled inside and dragged him out, the old man squealing in protest. Finally, the immigrants were herded toward the building. But while the Chinese man had staged his short-lived protest JoJo had slipped away into the shadows and run to a parked car a few hundred yards away. He was exhilarated but also confused, and he fearfully flattened himself on the cold concrete as an airplane roared overhead on takeoff. JoJo spoke only the limited English that Callahan had taught him. Except for the doctor, he knew no one in England, and at the moment, in his confused state, he had forgotten where he was. But at least for the moment, even though he was shivering from the unaccustomed cold, he felt like a bird taking flight. He was free! He was removed from the spectacle of starvation, of disease and death. A faint, unfamiliar sense of hope rose within him.

•   •   •

Still later that night, Nick Callahan descended the steps of the local police station where he had been booked for disturbing the peace. A stranger had paid his stiff fine. He huddled inside his leather jacket, thinking out his next move. A light snow had begun to fall. He knew that somehow he had to rescue JoJo and he knew that wouldn't be easy; the boy was already in the clutches of the British bureaucracy and in danger of being returned to Ethiopia without Callhan's protection—to certain death.

He was about to hail a cab when a stout man stepped out of the shadows and approached him. He wore a Russian fur cap pulled low across his eyebrows.

"Doctor Callahan," he said, "I'd like to have a word with you. The name's Jan Steiger." He extended his hand, but Callahan held back, studying the man warily.

"You're not a reporter, are you?"

"No. Far from it," Steiger replied. "I was there tonight, witnessing your fine moment."

He handed Callahan a business card: *The Egress Foundation* it said, in bold blue script, with locations in Washington D.C. and Geneva. Callahan stuck the card in his jacket and began to walk, Steiger falling in stride beside him.

"Egress," Callahan said, breaking the silence. "Sounds pretentious enough to be a charity. Am I right?" He turned and studied the short, swarthy man. "Oh wait—I remember you now. I was in

India—three, no, four years ago—and your lot were working the border with Afghanistan. The rumors were, you got in."

Steiger nodded, a smile curling his thin lips but not reaching his eyes.

"A lot of people are still dying over there," Callahan continued. "Nothing's been settled."

"People always do die, Doctor Callahan, as you well know. And things are rarely settled to everyone's satisfaction."

"Well, I'm no warrior," Callahan said. "That stuff leaves me cold. I'm in the relief business."

"I'm well aware of who you are and what you've accomplished," Steiger said. "You made a pretty emphatic statement at the Ball—no one is likely to forget it."

"I was angry. Sometimes my temper gets the better of me."

"So here we are, Doctor Callahan. You with your relief work and me with my relief work. Isn't that a strange coincidence?"

"I'm not sure I follow you."

"What I'm saying is, I need to get into Ethiopia and you're already there. You need money and I have money. Do you see what I mean?"

Callahan regarded the man and then slowly shook his head.

"No thanks."

"I'd fund your work, of course. Fund it generously."

"No."

Callahan turned away and started to walk, but Steiger stopped him with his voice.

"Let me quote you, Doctor. 'I've got a camp with thirty thousand people dying at a rate of forty a day. Six weeks from now, if I don't get help, they'll all be dead.' Your words, or very close to them." He waited until Callahan turned to stare at him; he wanted the man's full attention. "You were exaggerating, of course, but what you said was inherently true and very effective."

"Not an exaggeration," Callahan said quietly. "It's going to happen."

"Then all the more reason to accept my funding."

"Right—with about ten thousand strings attached."

"Money is money."

"I'll debate that with you another time. Some money is clean, some is dirty. More to the point, since when did the CIA start giving a shit about the starving in Africa?"

Callahan's hazel eyes remained fixed on the man's face, waiting for an answer. Steiger looked away. "Tell me something, Doctor Callahan—just idle curiosity on my part. Your performance tonight . . . was that a cry for help or a cry for attention?"

"I'd call it a press conference," Callahan

answered. "No. More like a declaration of independence."

"Freedom is an expensive commodity. You should see what I paid for your bail."

"No one asked you to bail me out."

"But I did."

Callahan shook his head. "No deal, Steiger. I don't play in your game."

Again he started to walk, and again the stout man fell into step beside him.

"Passion is cheap," he said. "You're an intelligent man. You know that the ends justify the means."

"You keep telling me what I know. What I know and what you know are two entirely different things. If you're looking for a dancing bear, try the fucking circus."

"I'm the best deal in town," Steiger said softly. "But if you insist on being stubborn, that's your choice. There are plenty more like you out there."

The following morning, Sarah stood in early dawn light, smoking, sipping coffee and gazing out the window. She was drawn deep into herself, feeling the weight of her half-forgotten dreams from the night before. The dark burning eyes of the young African boy haunted her now as they had haunted her dreams. There had been running, fighting, and bloodshed in her dreams—or in the one continuous dream, which she would awaken from and return to—and she stood on the sidelines, a helpless spectator, unable to intervene.

The television played softly, an early-morning news show, but she was oblivious to it. She sipped more coffee, hoping that it would bring her more thoroughly awake and help her to escape from the heavy mood of her dreams.

"Sis—good morning."

Charlotte appeared in the doorway, coat on and bag at her side.

"Cigarettes at dawn," she said. "You're either postcoital or you haven't slept."

"Morning, Charlie. Coffee?"

"No thanks."

"I'll call you a cab."

"I've called already." She examined her sister. "You do look like the wrath of God. A very pretty wrath, but even so . . ."

"I had a really lousy night's sleep."

"Which accounts for the cigarette—*not* postcoital."

"I'm afraid not, Miss Snoopy—not that it's any of your business."

Charlotte continued to stare at her sister. "Sarah?"

"Yes?"

"You're still brooding about last night. I know you. My advice is, forget about it. It was a stunt."

"I'm not so sure of that."

Charlotte glanced at her watch. "The cab's going to be here any minute. I wish I had the time to talk some horse sense into you."

"What do you mean?"

"I read you, li'l sis. I read you like a book. You have a tendency to take the weight of the world on your shoulders. That boy got to you."

"You heard what the doctor said, Charlie. The boy is going to die—and thousands more like him."

"Did it ever occur to you that the good doctor might be exaggerating?"

"I don't think he is."

Charlotte gave Sarah a hug and a kiss on the cheek. She knew it was time to change the subject. "Henry still sleeping?"

"Yes." Sarah pulled her sister close in another, tighter hug. "I wish you didn't have to go."

"I know, sweetie, but I promise not to stay away." She smiled. "If it all gets too stiff and English, give me a call. I'll send you some pretzels—no—macaroni and cheese, with a bottle of Dr Pepper. No, better yet—hair spray."

"Hair spray," Sarah repeated, managing a smile. "I like that."

The doorbell rang.

"Okay—that's me. Gotta go . . ." Charlotte reached for her. "Tell Henry, well, tell Henry . . . never mind . . . Just send him my—love? Warmest regards? Whatever they do here." She leaned forward to give her sister a kiss. "I love you."

"I love you, too," Sarah replied.

From the window she watched Charlotte climb into the cab and she did not move away until the cab turned a corner and disappeared from view. At that moment something on the TV caught her attention. A live report was in progress from a highway on the outskirts of London. She moved quickly to the set and sat within inches of it, her eyes widening. There was a blue flair of police cars and in the background loomed a large brick building. An airplane taking off filled the top of the screen.

The TV reporter said, ". . . The boy was found in the early hours of the morning here, under junction five. Initial reports, not yet confirmed, suggest that he died of hypothermia. A spokesman for the immigration department blamed the security lapse on staff shortages. The boy escaped from a police van as he and a number of other illegal aliens were being transferred to immigration authorities. We're told that the boy was arrested last night in a disturbance at a charity ball in a London hotel.

"A man identified as Nicholas Callahan, a physician presently doing relief work in Ethiopia, interrupted the proceedings of Aid Relief International to deliver an impassioned plea for additional help in Africa. It appears that the boy came into the country with Doctor Callahan, but details as to how and when are still not clear."

Sarah pressed the remote and the screen went dark. She sat without moving for at least five minutes, staring straight ahead sightlessly.

Later that morning, she stood beside her boss, Hubert Morley, at the Cartwright Gallery, where she was employed as a saleswoman. Morley was viewing a striking painting by Suzanne Dubuc, commenting on space, balance, and color to potential buyers, a wealthy middle-aged couple. Sarah, notebook in hand, appeared to be listening intently, but she knew the sales lecture by heart—each well-turned, erudite phrase. Her mind was a million miles away.

Morley, his manner sincere and intelligent, if slightly unctuous, said, "When Dubuc started, you could see how much she owed to van Gogh. She made no attempt to hide it—it's all encapsulated in her landscapes. But if you look here"—he extended a plump, well-manicured first finger—"what she's doing with this abstract . . . it's something more calculated and entirely different . . . more developed in the formal sense. The way she takes on the theme of attraction and repulsion—dark against light, opaque against the transparent . . . always searching for the balance. I think it's quite beautiful."

The wife nodded and gave a brief, polite smile. The husband scowled at the canvas as though confronting an adversary. And as Sarah, her notebook at her side, stared at the abstract piece in front of her, all she could see were the large and haunted eyes of a young African boy.

The art dealer said, "We have more of Dubuc's work from the middle period, if you would care to see it." He shot his cuff and sneaked a quick glance at his watch. "You'll have to excuse me a moment . . . Sarah, would you be so kind as to show Mr. and Mrs. Campbell other paintings in the back room?"

"I'm sorry, Hubert."

Sarah turned on her heel and walked into the office where Agatha Trail, the gallery's owner, was busy on the phone. She waited by the door until Miss Trail finished her conversation.

"I'm resigning, Agatha," Sarah said.

Miss Trail waved her to a chair. "Sit down, dear. Why would you do something silly like that? You're very good at what you do. Clients speak very highly of you." The older woman lit a strong French cigarette, filling her office with acrid blue smoke. "Trouble at home?"

"Not at all," Sarah answered, annoyed at the woman's intrusion into her private affairs. "It's just . . . I'm not happy. I feel as though I'm treading water."

"If you stay with me, I believe I can promise you a very exciting future." She hesitated, puffed on the vile cigarette. "Hubert, you know, is near retirement."

"I'm sorry," Sarah said, rising. "I've made up my mind. I'm giving notice. Would two weeks be appropriate so that you can find a replacement?"

Miss Trail also rose and put out her cigarette with a vicious jab. "As far as I'm concerned," she said, "you can clear out your desk today."

Sarah sipped a glass of very expensive Bordeaux, brought up by her husband from the Bauford wine cellar, and stared back at Henry, her jaw clenched. She sensed his bewilderment and hurt, but she was determined not to give into it. She wasn't going to let him talk her around to his point of view. Not this time. She was certain that you had only so many chances to steer your life in the right direction, and this was one of those times. She hated hurting her husband, but she knew that if she backed down now she would hurt him more deeply in the end.

"Sweetheart, are you sure you know what you're doing?"

"Yes, Henry."

"But this is so spur of the moment. You could even call it impetuous."

"Maybe you could, but you would be wrong. This is what I've always been looking for. I just didn't realize it until I saw that child at the Ball and saw how to many people his life is no more important than a common household fly. But he's a human being—or was. People like him need help." Sarah smiled. She touched Henry's hand, which was cold and unresponsive. "I didn't mean to give a speech. Sorry."

"We've only been married a few months, Sarah. I rather thought that during this period—

the honeymoon phase—we'd spend our time together."

"But we don't," she said. "You have your work. You're gone all day. I have idle time on my hands."

"You had the art gallery job. But you quit it."

"The work was meaningless. I need meaning in my life, just as you do."

"But there are many professionals trained to do relief work. What do you think you can contribute?"

Sarah fought against a growing sense of resentment. "You seem to be saying I have nothing to offer."

"Not at all. To the contrary. It's just that—"

"Do you think you married a stupid girl?"

"That's just ridiculous, Sarah. I couldn't possibly marry someone who wasn't clever."

"But I'm not a trophy either. Something to put on the shelf and show off to your friends on special occasions."

"I know that, and I never suggested any such thing."

Sarah sensed that she had finally maneuvered Henry into a corner. He was beginning to stutter nervously and look distinctly ill at ease. Now was the time to strike.

"Before you say anything more, I've spoken to all the relevant relief organizations. With forty thousand pounds—"

"Forty thousand pounds?" he interrupted.

"Let me finish, please."

He started to say something, but then, with visible effort, remained silent.

"With forty thousand pounds," she repeated, "I can buy food and supplies from surplus regions in Southern Sudan. From there I can transport them into Tigre. I've maxed my credit cards and found a buyer for my car. But I'm still short about twelve thousand."

Henry waited until he was certain that she had come to a pause, then said quietly, "Sarah, that isn't how it's done. You need P.O.W., you know, to be successful."

"And what is P.O.W.?" she said, trying to control her impatience.

"Planning, organization, and workers," Henry said. "One doesn't just jump into these things with deep pockets and a kind heart."

"Patronizing," Sarah mumbled.

"What?"

"You're patronizing me."

"Not at all. I'm simply stating some hard facts."

They stared at each other until Sarah said, "I've made up my mind, Henry."

"I can see that." He sighed and looked away.

"I love you," she said. "But I have to do this."

Henry took a sip of wine, swirled it in his mouth, swallowed slowly. "Then send the money. Do charitable work. Mother does."

"I'm not your mother."

"Do whatever to help the cause," he hurried on. "But please don't go roaming off to some god-forsaken hole in Africa to salve your conscience."

"Salve my conscience?" Her tone was quiet and dangerous.

"Maybe I'm not putting it quite right."

"Maybe you're not."

"But I do feel . . . I can't help but say that it's simply not a grown-up way to behave."

"Then maybe I don't want to be a grown-up—not quite yet anyway."

Henry contemplated Sarah with a sinking sensation in the pit of his stomach. She was so heartbreakingly beautiful, he loved her so very much, and he was terrified of losing her. More than anything, he wanted her to be happy. He wanted them to live a long life together, have children, travel, and grow old together. In his secret heart Henry did not feel deserving of her. He knew that she was cleverer than he was. He had always discounted his looks as an unearned attribute, and often when he was at his happiest—standing beside Sarah at a party admiring her intelligence and beauty—he would feel a sudden chill. *She's too good for me. I will never understand why she chose me when she could have had anyone.*

"All right," he said, reaching for her hand. "If that's what you want, fine. You know I'd never stand in your way."

"It is what I want, Henry. It's what I *need.*" She smiled and kissed him lightly on the lips.

"I'll help you find the money."

"Thank you. You have no idea how much that means to me."

"I can talk to father. He knows literally everybody. Mind you, Ethiopia is a bit of a . . . it's rather, well, primitive and—"

"I know what Ethiopia is, Henry," she said shortly. "Your father has given me a through briefing at many a dinner."

"Yes, of course. Fine. As you know, his network is vast. We'll find the money."

"I appreciate your help," she said.

"Well, after all, you're my wife. Father told me that your first duty in life is to make the woman you marry happy."

"Your father is a very wise man."

"I know."

Her gentle irony had completely passed him by. She squeezed his arm and said, "You are the sweetest thing. Do you want to come with me? It would be wonderful if we could share this experience."

Henry stared at her, looking truly bewildered. He cleared his throat a number of times before saying, "My love, that's the most . . . that's quite wonderful. I'm so touched that you would want me along. But even if I could . . ." He shrugged, looked away.

She chewed the corner of her lip and shook her head slightly. "You're saying you can't—or won't?"

"It's not that, Sarah. You know me. I'm not cut out for this kind of venture. I'm not a man of action—a James Bond. Not by a long stretch. I'm a city person. I need four walls and a comfy bed, three meals a day and cocktails before dinner."

"I think you're braver than you know," she said.

"Perhaps so. Though truthfully I rather doubt it. But brave or not, I have meetings lined up for the next month. This is our busiest time, you know." He held her hand. "You go. You have the right attitude and the passion for this sort of thing."

Sarah had known when she married Henry that there was a soft core at the center of him and a willingness to let others do the heavy lifting. He had told her a story about an Oxford classmate who had been expelled for cheating on an exam. Henry, along with many others, had been questioned. Although under pressure he did not accuse his friend of cheating, he did refuse to exonerate him. "Clive did cheat, after all," Henry explained to Sarah. "Some of the others straight-out lied for him, risking their own academic careers. But my feeling was, he brought it on himself and he would have to pay the consequences."

"I think I would lie for a friend," Sarah responded. "Everyone is entitled to a mistake."

"Perhaps so," Henry said. "But is it worth the risk of getting in trouble yourself?" Worth the risk . . . That was the man she had married: a man who calculated his comfort and avoided risks. He gave little trouble, accepted as little complexity as possible, and steered the safe course. That was his way, but not her way.

"Look," she said, "I know this seems—well, little Miss Bleeding Heart and all that means. I know that about me. I was the little girl who wanted to save the world, take in every stray dog and cat and sad person in our neighborhood, and I guess I haven't changed. I know who I am and I just don't care. I realize you think I'm crazy, and—and I understand that you can't come with me . . . I'm just saying—oh my God, am I crying? Just see me off at the airport. That's all I ask."

"Of course, my darling."

"You do think I'm crazy, don't you?"

"I think you're brave. Generous. The perfect woman."

"Oh, Henry . . ."

He took her in his arms and kissed her deeply, his eyes closed. She returned his kiss fervently, her eyes wide open. Her eyes saw the future. They saw the world opening.

Ethiopia, riven by civil war, by despotic regimes, by drought and disease and starvation, still struck Sarah as a profoundly beautiful land. Perhaps part of the attraction was the strangeness of a country so different from England with its gentle green pastures and cozy hills and hamlets. She sensed its immensity along with its danger. She loved the long vistas empty of trees, vegetation, and life. But most of all, she loved the feeling that for the first time in her life she was risking herself for a purpose that was larger than her own existence. Great Britain represented safety and privilege—the unearned life. Now, thrust into the vortex of a world aching and unhinged, she was ready to test her wings, to soar.

A convoy of two ten-ton trucks, followed by two water tankers, rumbled down the dirt road, cutting a swath of dust across a wasteland of caked riverbeds and dead trees. Tula, the driver of the lead truck, a small, wiry black woman, chattered away to Sarah as she drove with one hand and held a small ropelike cigar in the other. She was in her late twenties but looked closer to forty. She was among the few fortunate Ethiopian women who had received the equivalent of a high school education and had mastered a working knowledge of the English language. Her husband had been shot in a tribal skirmish a few years earlier, leaving her with four children to support. Sarah was fascinated by Tula's tales, and was unaware of the sweat salting her eyes and face. As she listened, she stared at the lunar landscape, glimpsed through amber dust clouds, with a mixture of awe and apprehension.

Tula, speaking rapidly, said, "Three years and no rain. Not a drop. That and war. My husband and my four brothers, all dead. People leave their homes and wander. There is nothing for them. We have now ten camps on the south side—Korem, Mekele, Lalibela, Waldiya, Adwa. . . ."

As Tula talked on, Sarah stared at long lines of families walking along the roadside, moving slowly, mostly silent, dust-covered processions. The convoy rumbled past corpses laid out on the roadside rolled in straw mats. Dark clouds of flies hovered over them. Alongside the corpses, oblivious to them, older people squatted, unable to move. The more fortunate ones sat beneath pieces of canvas and cloth tied to a pole, warding off the withering sun. They looked seriously ill, stretched thin and taut to the edge of death. The younger and stronger refugees, still able to walk, lined the sides of the road like numbed robots.

"Where are they going?" Sarah asked.

"Nowhere," Tula replied. "That is God's truth. They have nowhere to go. But at least they are moving, and moving gives some hope."

Sarah stared in horror at a young man whose facial skin was half gone.

"Measles," Tula said, following her glance. "You know measles?"

"Yes, of course."

"Measles a curse. It kill you here. Many die. No vaccine."

Sarah made a gesture toward the back of the truck. "We brought some medicines that—"

"Also cholera everywhere," Tula went on, either not hearing or not believing Sarah. "We dig very deep now to find good water. It is rare—like gold. Starvation everywhere. Death is everywhere."

They drove for a moment in silence. Sarah's eyes filled with unforgettable images of desolation.

"You speak English very well," she said presently.

"Missionaries teach me. They say I have ability. I learn fast."

"Are you married again? Do you have a man?"

Tula gave a sharp bark of laughter. "No man now. Most of the men, they no damn good. They beg to marry me—many, many times. I drive truck, and they know I make money. I am my own boss. Lazy man good for nothing. I work to take care of my children, not to have no man live off me. Don't need to take care of no man." Tula drove on in silence, then added more quietly, "Me too old now, anyway. It is just my money they after. My beauty is gone. They take my money and marry girl fourteen."

"Men," Sarah said in sympathy.

Her eyes were drawn to the sight of an emaciated child, glimpsed through drifting clouds of dust beyond the line of walking refugees. As Sarah stared, the child tried to move, one hand slightly raised, fluttering feebly.

Sarah touched the sleeve of Tula's jacket. "Stop," she said.

"Cannot stop now," Tula answered. She shook her head, staring straight ahead.

"Stop the truck!" Sarah cried out, her voice conveying an urgent strength that Tula could not ignore.

Tula reluctantly hit the brakes, grinding to a halt. "You leave this alone," she muttered sullenly. "This is wrong."

Sarah hopped out of the truck and moved quickly through the refugees, fiercely determined, up the slope toward the mother and child. As she drew closer she saw a vulture, wings pulsating slowly in the still air, waiting patiently no more than ten yards away. Waiting for the smell that told it the prey was ready to be devoured. Without thinking, Sarah grabbed up a rock and flung it at the predator. It flapped quickly away, only to wait a little farther off. Ever vigilant, maintaining its vigil of death.

Hesitantly, half repulsed, Sarah stepped up and, arms outstretched, lifted the child in an awkward embrace. She held her breath against the terrible stench and felt on her breast the feverish heat emanating from the child. Nearly lifeless in her arms, the child uttered a faint moan. The mother lay nearby, a festering wound on her abdomen, oozing pus. She muttered weakly to Sarah in Tigreyan.

"What is she saying?" Sarah called to Tula.

"Her name is Gemilla. The boy, his name is Abraha."

Gemilla continued to talk and Tula reluctantly translated. "She say that she is dying. She want you to bring the child to her."

Sarah carried the child to Gemilla, who kissed him gently on each eyelid. The dying mother stared up at Sarah and whispered in Tigreyan, her eyes blazing with an urgent appeal. This time

Sarah did not need the words interpreted: Their message was clear. She had to save the boy.

"No," Tula shouted. She was out of the truck and waving frantically from the side of the road. "No woman! No baby!"

Sarah did not answer but continued toward the truck, holding the baby in both arms.

"No, *no,*" Tula said. "We go. You know nothing about this. Leave child with its mother. You do wrong thing here."

Sarah, in a state of shock, simply stared at the woman. She stood beside the truck, listening to her but barely comprehending.

"We go. *Now,*" Tula hissed.

Sarah continued staring, her eyes fixed. She held a dying child in her arms as an enraged woman she had just met screamed at her, and the child's mother lay dying in the dirt beside the road. It was a nightmare but a real nightmare, and after the first flush of shock, Sarah felt deep within herself a growing stubbornness, a reluctance to bend to the African woman's will.

"If the child stays here, I stay."

"This is wrong," Tula shouted. "You know nothing, woman child."

"The mother comes, too," Sarah said. "Lift her into the truck."

"You don't know nothing. You say things and what do you know? You listen to Tula now."

"Do what I say."

With dark mutterings in Tigreyan, Tula picked up Gemilla, showing surprising strength for a woman of such slight stature, and laid her, not gently, atop sacks of grain in the back of the truck. At Sarah's insistence, she then bound Gemilla's wound with a ripped-up T-shirt.

They drove on, and Tula, in the grip of her anger, accelerated too quickly, the truck bucking as it hit the potholes in the road. They could hear Gemilla groaning from the force of each bounce. Sarah held Abraha in her arms, staring straight ahead, her face set in grim lines. She felt that she could throw up from the gut repulsion to the filth, the swarming flies, but she was determined not to show any weakness in front of this woman. She would die first.

Tula was seething with anger and making no attempt to hide it. She chattered a steady stream under her breath as she gripped the wheel; she no longer made the slightest effort to avoid the pot-holes.

"Slow down," Sarah said, breaking the silence.

"I am the driver of this truck, woman."

"I said slow down."

After a moment Tula eased her foot off the accelerator and went on the attack.

"Is a waste," she said. "Child and mother . . . both a waste."

"I don't think so. And anyway, that's for me to decide."

"Stupid baby woman. You come here—you come to my land—knowing nothing. One day here, you use your mouth, not your eyes to see this land. You only make many problems."

Sarah said nothing. For her, the conversation was closed.

The two women, both stubborn, neither willing to give an inch, exchanged venomous stares. They drove the rest of the way to the refugee camp in silence.

The truck began overheating, steam pouring out of the hood, just as they approached the entrance to the camp. Tula stepped down and asked the driver of the truck behind to fill the radiator while she checked the oil gauge. When she was about to climb back into the cabin, she saw that the child Abraha had been neatly nestled inside Sarah's jacket on the seat but that Sarah had disappeared.

"Shit," Tula cried out angrily. "Where the baby woman go?"

She stormed up to the driver of the truck parked behind her, his motor idling. "Where that white woman go?" she said in Tigreyan. "You seen her?"

"Walking toward the camp," he answered with a nod of his head. "Walk fast." He grinned. "Fancy white lady."

Tula shielded her eyes, using her hand as a visor against the sun, and tried to spot the

American woman. All around her families were continuing to advance along the roadside toward the camp. She ignored them, pushing them aside when they came too close.

Sarah's progress was slowed by the crowds of people as she walked up the gentle rise toward the camp. She had tried so hard to control her temper, to reason with the African woman, but her emotions had overwhelmed her. She wondered what was wrong with Tula. Didn't she have any feelings for her own people? She had been perfectly willing to leave the woman and child beside the road to die. How could anyone be that callow, that heartless?

As she walked up the rise, still seething, salt burning her eyes, her thoughts turned to Henry. His last letter had sounded so dispirited; he was like a child who had been abandoned by his mother. The letter had left Sarah feeling edgy and annoyed. He seemed to be clinging to her for emotional sustenance, and that seemed to her unseemly and unnatural in a grown man. It was bad for them both. She hadn't yet answered his letter; she wasn't sure how to respond. She wanted to say, Buck up, Henry, be a man, make me proud, and don't lean on me too much. But that would hurt him when what he needed most of all was reassurance. She was beginning to sense her husband's frailty. It was not a pleasant feeling.

She was suddenly aware of a faint droning

sound. She turned and scrambled up a cluster of rocks that burned her through the soles of her shoes. The droning grew louder. At the top of the rise she could see a huge valley, sun scorched and devoid of growth, stretching for nearly a mile. The refugee camp lay directly below her.

Lulled by the droning sound, which had grown more frenzied and rhythmic, Sarah began to descend, moving cautiously down a bed of jagged rocks. There was a kind of reverence to the sound now, a form of religious chanting, certain words repeated over and over again. It was then that Sarah understood she was listening to the sound of human beings, the sound of misery, of masses of people raising their voices to the heavens. The land below her writhed with the swaying of their many bodies. Sarah stared, mesmerized. She was amazed and stunned that she had lived nearly twenty-four years in this world and really had seen nothing at all. Tula is right, she thought. I am a stupid baby woman.

Slowly she began her return to the truck. She was concerned that Tula might, in her absence, abandon the mother and child by the side of the road. She heard the rumble of engines, and figuring the truck was ready to move, she broke into a trot. But the hood was still up, and Tula was pacing back and forth muttering to herself angrily. At that moment three jeeps squealed to a stop in a curtain of dust on the road next to the trucks. A group of TPLF rebels hopped out carrying AK-47s. Bandoliers were strapped across their chests and they carried broad-bladed knives in scabbards made of hide. The rebel leader, a slender youth with wild black hair twisted into braids and a long scar down his cheek, shoved one of the truck drivers aside with the butt of his rifle and gestured to his men to unload the trucks. Tula rushed forward shaking her fists and screeching at the rebel leader in Tigreyan. He pushed her off like an annoying gnat but she kept coming back at him.

Sarah yelled, "Don't, Tula. They'll hurt you."

"Stay back, lady," Tula said without looking at her. Cursing at the leader, she twisted out of his grasp and grabbed a rebel by the waist and spun him around. She tried to wrestle a bag from his hand as they staggered in a circle like two drunks dancing. The bag fell to the ground, splitting open, and a shower of beans spilled across the roadside.

"Abraha," Sarah said out loud and rushed toward the truck, but before she could reach the passenger door she was knocked off balance by a wave of refugees descending on the spilled beans. Another blow—a hard elbow to her ribs—staggered her. She sank to the ground and was kicked and trampled on repeatedly as people ran over her. Through blinding pain in her chest and head she somehow managed to crawl the few feet to the truck, reach up and open the door. She pulled herself up and dove inside. Abraha was sleeping fitfully, his breathing fast and shallow. Choking back bile of fear and pain, Sarah touched his forehead. It was scalding hot and his skin felt like dry parchment.

"You poor sick child," she whispered, running a hand over his hair. "My baby . . ."

She watched from the safety of the truck as a mass of refugees crawled, wrestled and fought to capture a few beans, for every last granule of food. Others in swarms attacked the rebels, grabbing bags from them, ripping and shredding them. More beans, more fighting, screaming, and chaos. The rebels, woefully outmanned, began beating people with their rifle butts and bandoliers. Shots were fired into the air to try to dispel the crowd, but nothing deterred them. There was food to be had, and it was clear from watching them struggle that food was the most important thing on earth. Sarah had never thought of food and water in those terms; that in the end they were the only two things that mattered in life. These swarms of people would get to the beans or die trying. Watching them, Sarah knew that if they didn't eat something very soon most of them would not live out the week. That doctor—Nick Callahan—he hadn't exaggerated. He hadn't been grandstanding. This was hell on earth, and Sarah, holding a dying child in her arms, was right in the midst of it.

Her face pressed against the window, she

blinked at the fury of dust and writhing humanity encircling her. Instinctively, she cradled Abraha more tightly, rocking him, crooning to him. Her worried glance sought out Tula, but the African woman had disappeared in the crowd. Then her eye caught the rebel leader as he raised his rifle and fired directly into the crowd. A scream went up and the refugees began to scatter at the same moment that a jeep roared to a screeching halt directly in front of the truck. The rebels turned, weapons cocked and aimed. The leader raised an arm and shouted something—obviously calling for calm as the soldiers slowly lowered their rifles. Nick Callahan leaped out and plowed into the crowd, a huge African everyone called Ribs running interference for him. Ribs, the doctor's bodyguard and general assistant, wore a bright yellow turban. He was built like an NFL lineman, and everyone respected his size. No one was fooled by his mild manner. If need be, he would gladly kill for Callahan. He shouldered everyone out of the way, creating a clear path for the doctor. An American, Elliot Hauser, gingerly stepped out of the backseat of the jeep and followed after them. His pale face beneath his pith helmet was tight with concern. Dangling from his neck was a Buddhist emblem in the form of a knot of eternity. Ribs shoved aside a haughty-looking rebel who had said something to him, a nasty leer twisting his lips.

Callahan rapidly approached Tula, who had suddenly reappeared and was screaming at the rebel leader.

"Shut up," he told her as he stared at the leader. She quickly fell silent. Callahan walked up to the leader and they stared at each other in silence. Sarah, gazing at them through the side window, clutched Abraha close to her breast. The two men, she thought, resembled warring dogs taking the measure of each other.

"Meles," Callahan said quietly. "This is not right. You know better than this, man."

The leader shrugged, his dark eyes fixed on Callahan's face. Meles's men stood ready, weapons cocked, waiting for a signal. Sarah realized that the doctor could be dead in an instant. She held her breath, felt her heart pound, but could not look away.

"I'll give you four bags," Callahan said.

"Four bags not enough, medicine man," Meles answered. "Need one truck."

There was a subtle shift in the mood; the rebels, even though they did not understand the language, seemed to sense that their leader and the white man were in the process of negotiating. They were talking, their voices were calm. The crowd of refugees hovering around the perimeter was quiet, waiting.

Callahan gestured toward the refugees. "Come on, Meles, be reasonable. You want to tell them you're taking half of their food? How many are you? Fifty? A hundred? There are thousands of them."

"My men fight for them. . . ."

"I know, I know. You fight for the people. You struggle against their oppressors." He lowered his voice. "But Meles, there's something I don't understand. Maybe you can explain it to me. You fired into them. A woman is lying there dead. From the bullets in your rifle. You are a clever general. Why did you do that?"

"We were threatened."

"By these poor people? How could that be? They have no weapons. They are sick, starving people. They can hardly stand on their feet."

"I want one truck," Meles repeated. His expression remained menacing and dark, but he had lowered his voice.

Callahan glanced at Elliot Hauser, who stepped forward with a large box and some smaller cartons wrapped in brown paper.

"I've got some other presents for you, Meles," he said. "You know I try to honor your needs."

"I don't need no presents from you," the rebel leader replied, although he looked at the packages with interest. "I take one truck. That is my demand."

Callahan smiled, unfazed.

Sarah, watching them, no longer felt they resembled angry dogs. They were more like two chess masters possessed of powerful and equal skills involved in some pivotal match. The outcome of the game, though, the winning or the losing, might prove fatal. They stood there calmly, plotting moves, working out strategy while many lives hung in the balance. She felt helpless; never in her life had she been less in charge of her fate.

Two women would do it differently, she thought. They would seek common ground. They would talk it through and find peaceful solutions without the strutting and the subterfuge.

"Cigarettes," Callahan said suddenly. "You like Camels, don't you, Meles? The best cigarette there is. Made in America. I've got six cartons for you and your men. For your fine group of revolutionaries."

"Camel cigarettes," Meles repeated almost dreamily, staring at the cartons.

"That's right," Callahan said.

Then he shouted at the rebels in Tigreyan, gesturing, ordering them to return the bags of food and supplies to the trucks. His voice was forceful, commanding, deep. Some, reluctantly, started to return the bags until Meles ordered them to stop. The two men had reached another impasse. The rebel leader, drilling Callahan with his dark eyes, held out his hand. Callahan reached into a bag and brought out half a dozen *Playboy* magazines. For the first time Meles grinned. His face, Sarah thought, had become suddenly radiant and beautiful.

"Twelve bags, Callahan," he said. Beginning the next stage of the bargaining.

"That's too many."

"Better for you than one truck."

"Be reasonable, Meles. I offer four, you ask for twelve. Think of how many mouths those extra bags will feed. These are your people. You are fighting for their freedom. The weak can never overthrow their oppressors."

The rebel leader listened and after a long silence said, "Four bags each truck. Eight bags. This is fair, yes?"

Callahan gave him a noncommital glance. Meles then turned to Hauser. "This is fair, Mr. Elliot, yes? This is fair. We bargain."

Elliot exchanged a look with Callahan, who finally nodded. Callahan then turned to Tula and said, "Get the bags down from the truck. Let's get out of here."

He turned back to Meles and said, "Don't ever fire into these people again. I'm surprised at you, Meles. You are a clever general of your people."

"They threatened us."

"Save your bullets for the oppressors."

Without another word, Meles strutted off with his men. Callahan strolled up to the truck Sarah was sitting in and rapped on the window. She lowered it a few inches.

"Welcome to famine relief," he said, a tight smile on his face. But the smile didn't reach his eyes. They were cold—and definitely unwelcoming.

Before she could reply, he was gone.

J oss Newcombe was indispensable to Callahan and Hauser. A tall rugged Australian in his mid-thirties, Newcombe was a man of many talents: he could do carpentry, plumbing, and electrical wiring, he spoke decent Tigreyan (only Elliot was more fluent); and he had the respect of the rebel faction. Newcombe had earned a degree in electrical engineering, but when his marriage ended badly he made the decision to travel the world and use his many talents in the service of aid relief. An unpretentious man with a rough, take-no-prisoners sense of humor, a big beer drinker and an expert spinner of tall tales, he had gravitated naturally to Callahan. They both detested the status quo and abhorred falsity and greed in whatever forms they took. They were brothers under the skin.

As Callahan drove into the main compound in a swirl of dust, leading the four-truck convoy, Joss was standing over a drilling rig, surrounded by a team of African helpers. He was making an adjustment to the cable tension, the drill grinding away with a slightly irregular beat, when there was a sudden jolt and the machinery shuddered to a halt.

Joss tossed a large wrench to the ground and scowled at the rig. "Shit," he muttered, "the blasted thing's broken again." He turned to his assistant, a slender African with an alert, intelligent face. "Looks like the Gods are against us again, mate."

"We can fix."

"You're an optimist," Joss said with a wry grin. He watched Callahan climb out of the jeep and gave him a thumbs-down.

"Jesus, not again," Callahan said.

"Afraid so."

"When are we going to catch a break?" Callahan lit a cigarette and glared at the drill.

Joss gestured toward his assistant. "Ask Hugh here. He's the eternal optimist."

"We fix," Hugh said, grinning.

Sarah studied the details of camp life as the truck came to a halt—the incredible squalor, the stench of human degradation, the hundreds of gaunt faces, sick and dying, staring at her with enormous saucer eyes. Flies landed on their faces and they made no attempt to shoo them away. The flies were a fact of life like disease, starvation, and early death. When nothing could be done, nothing was attempted.

"We here, lady," Tula said grimly. "You get out now."

But Sarah made no move. She observed the camp's main square. Encircling it were makeshift huts, miscellaneous storage facilities, a transportation pool, and three broken-down buildings that passed for a hospital. Beyond them was a crumbling brick building that had once served as a church. The sun beat down fiercely and images rippled and swayed before Sarah's eyes. She was filled with a sense of dread mixed with exhilaration.

"We are here," Tula said again. She cast a disapproving look at Abraha. Avoiding her eyes, Sarah wrapped the child more tightly in the fold of her jacket and climbed down from the truck.

As she stood in the square, Newcombe squinted through the sun at her. He whistled in approval.

"Who's the angel?" he said.

Callahan snorted. "Florence Nightingale come to tend the flock. She's out to save the world."

Joss observed his friend closely. "Well, is that such a bad thing, mate?"

"We'll see," Callahan said, and he didn't look happy.

"Back to the fuckin' drill," Joss said. "There's work to do."

"Good luck." Callahan started away.

"Hey—Nick?"

Callahan turned with a questioning frown.

"Be easy on the lady," Joss said, grinning. "She looks sort of fragile. Like some kind of exotic flower." He hesitated. "Give her a chance, okay, mate?"

"Concentrate on the drill, Joss. That's our priority."

He crossed the square toward the prefab storage areas. Elliot Hauser was standing nearby, ready to oversee the unloading of the trucks.

Sarah watched Callahan warily, sensing his mood. Steeling herself, she approached him. "Excuse me," she said.

Callahan stopped and looked straight into her eyes for a moment, then his eyes lingered on the baby. His face registered no expression.

A cool mask, she thought. The same look he had when he negotiated with that rebel leader— an expression you couldn't possibly read. I wonder if he practices it in the mirror.

"What is it," he said. He checked his watch with slow deliberation. "I'm busy."

"Um . . . this child . . . His mother's in the truck . . . she's seriously wounded . . . they both need immediate attention." She hated herself for stumbling over her words like a frightened school-girl.

She waited for a response. He continued to stare at her. Then, without warning, he turned from her and walked away. He marched off to the back of the truck, where Gemilla was being helped down by Tula and the driver of the second truck. Callahan leaned close to the woman and briefly examined her wounds. He nodded to Tula—some kind of silent communication, Sarah decided, feeling a surge of resentment—and the African woman returned his nod.

He walked back to Sarah and briefly examined the child in her arms.

"Too late," he said.

"I'm sorry. What did you say?" She forced herself to keep her voice steady.

"It's too late," he repeated. "As in, no point."

Sarah returned his stare steadily, calmly. Her fear—or awe—of him was beginning to fade.

"Why? I don't understand why it's too late. They're still alive."

Her forceful response was unexpected. Callahan was not used to having his decisions and judgments questioned. He ran the show his way, and brooked no interference. Even Elliot Hauser, nominally his superior, deferred to him on camp protocol, reserving to himself only the financial and fund-raising side of the operation.

Callahan blinked, sensing an impending conflict. He fought to control his temper. A skillful manipulator of people and situations, he was concerned that a show of anger would give her an advantage. Ribs, Elliot, Tula, and others gathered unobtrusively to watch this little war of wills play out.

"You ask why?" he said with a caustic smile. He let the smile stretch, trying to shake her resolve. "Well . . . quite apart from any illnesses they have—and I can't begin to count them—they're far too weak to survive."

"How do you know? Are you an expert on survival?"

"I happen to be the doctor here, Mrs. Bauford."

"But what gives you the right to decide? Miracles are always happening."

"There are no miracles here. We deal in what is called triage. My job is to make the tough decisions. I'm responsible for thousands of refugees."

"I heard that already . . . in London."

Callahan stared at her, temporarily at a loss for words. He did not like to be reminded of London. London was disgrace, London was the loss of JoJo. London meant far too many sleepless nights of depression and guilt.

"I know you were there," he said quietly. "You heard me speak. And everything I said that night was true."

"I believe you, Doctor Callahan. And I still think you should look at this baby and his mother."

"You do, do you?"

"Yes. I'm not here to tell you your job, but as a doctor I think it's your duty."

His face had turned crimson and his hands were trembling. He knew that he was losing it.

"Okay," he said, his voice deeper, raspier. "I see. It's all perfectly clear to me . . . Mrs. Bauford. You paid for the use of these trucks. You paid for the food, the medicine. So I have to indulge some white-arse idea of heroism, right? Hey . . . why stop there? I can get you a picture—in color, if you want. Would you like to have a picture as a souvenir? Here's a great shot—'Poor little rich girl holds dying black baby . . .' That should wow all your little white rich friends back home. You do your hair right, you'll look just great."

Sarah stood absolutely still. Even after such ferocious provocation she refused to crumble. She would not give him the satisfaction of anger or tears. If he could be cold, so could she. Her nerves fluttered, but she knew that they didn't show on the outside. She wanted more than anything to scream at him, but there was no way she was backing down now. She saw Tula's triumphant expression fixed on her and she forced a smile.

She said to Callahan, measuring each syllable, "I saw the child from the truck. He was struggling to breathe. I picked him up. His mother was wounded. I brought her here, too. Now please look at them."

Callahan held her level gaze, and for the first time began to have doubts about his ability to control her. He felt his authority slipping. He flashed Elliot a quick glance as though to say, Help me here. But his friend gave a slight shrug.

"Seems fair enough, Nick," he said softly.

Callahan looked away and studied the ground at his feet. He felt isolated. Why the hell had this woman come into his life and invaded his world? So sure of herself, so helplessly naïve . . . so beautiful . . . He felt that his staff, with the possible exceptions of Ribs and Tula, was taking satisfaction from this scene. He knew that he was squirming, suddenly at a disadvantage, and he had no idea how to take control back from this obstinate young woman.

He said quickly, "Okay, fine. I'll look at them. Ribs—take the baby. Tula, get the mother in hospital. All right now, let's get this stuff unloaded."

He shot Hauser a dark look, turned on his heel and stormed toward the storage area, muttering curses under his breath. Ribs stepped up, looming more than a foot above Sarah, and took the boy in his arms. He whispered to the child in his native singsong dialect as he smiled at Sarah. He spoke to her in Tigreyan.

Sarah turned to Tula. "What did he say?"

"He say you kind lady," Tula answered without meeting her eyes.

"Thank you," she said to the giant, returning his smile.

Tula and a helper carried Gemilla toward the makeshift hospital.

Across the compound, Hauser caught up with Callahan.

"Thanks for your help, friend," Callahan said. "Come crunch time I know who I can really depend on."

"Come on, Nick, spare me the sarcasm. She's a donor. There's no point in pissing off the money. We need every bit of help we can get."

"She sashays in here like Florence Fucking Nightingale and thinks she's about to save the world," Callahan said, still fuming, embarrassed by his curious and unusual loss of face. "Give me a break."

"Nick—"

"It's bullocks!" he exploded. "She marries the big shot's son and thinks she's queen of the universe."

"My guess is, she's in shock," Elliot said. "This is all new to her and she's trying to cope."

"Yeah, right. Cope. Trying to cope. The poor thing. Of course I should've expected you to be soft on her. You bloody Venice Beach Buddhists are all alike."

With that, Callahan turned and walked away. Behind him, staring at his retreating back, Hauser was smiling. He felt that in his own odd way his friend Nick was conceding that maybe there was a role for this woman to play after all, but being Nick, he couldn't bring himself to admit it.

Later that day, Hauser led Sarah through the compound toward the crumbling brick building that had once been a church. They were accompanied by Tula. There was still marked tension between the two women. Sarah was beginning to suspect that the African woman idolized Callahan—perhaps was half in love with him.

Elliot Hauser said, "Okay, so let me properly introduce myself. I'm the chief administrator and logistician—if that doesn't sound overly pompous. And then we have Nick, who's our team leader and full-time doctor." He cleared his throat and smiled. "He—as you can see, he has a lot on his hands right now."

Sarah returned his smile. "Yes. Thank you, by the way. . . ."

Hauser frowned, puzzled. "Sorry?"

"For what you said back there. Dr. Callahan is very . . . forceful. I felt overwhelmed."

Clearly uncomfortable with the drift of the conversation, Hauser said, "Oh—that's fine." He quickly moved on, saying, "So . . . these are our feeding stations. Low tech, but effective—like the rest of us. Our one goal is just to plow ahead and get the job done."

Sarah smiled. She was instinctively drawn to this gentle individual; his self-deprecating shyness and quiet irony reminded her of Henry. She felt a sudden stab of guilt when she thought of her husband and realized how seldom he had crossed her mind since she left London.

She said, "The food supplies we brought. How long will they last?"

"Ten to twelve days," he answered. "That is, if we ration responsibly."

"That's all?"

"Well, possibly we can stretch it to two weeks." He hesitated. "Again, it's a matter of triage. Those facing imminent death will be the last to be fed." Anticipating a reaction from her he shrugged and added, "I'm afraid that's the reality of life in refugee camps."

"But logically shouldn't the dying be the first to be fed?"

Elliot took a moment to answer. He liked this woman; she was beautiful and she seemed to be very intelligent and caring, but she had to be handled with caution. She was an important donor with intense feelings about the sanctity of life. He shared her feelings, but the years he had spent in refugee camps had brought a measure of hard-earned realism.

"If we feed those who are sure to die, then

someone who might live is more likely to die. I hate to put it this way, but we have to do the math with people's lives." He could tell that she wasn't happy with this line of argument; her eyes widened with skepticism and she pursed her lips. "We do the best we can, Mrs. Bauford, given the circumstances. At best this is a tragic business."

She nodded slowly. "What do you do if the food runs out?"

"Oh, we usually find a way." He tried to keep his tone light. "It's the same old problem—money, or the lack of it. . . . But with help we get by. We could always do with more, of course. . . ." He was gently angling for whatever she might have to offer (it was his job as administrator), and he knew that she knew what he was doing. But he felt no embarrassment; the situation was desperate and he was perfectly willing to prostrate himself and beg.

"What do you need most?" she asked, her tone suddenly businesslike.

"Vaccines," he answered. "No doubt about it. That's our number one priority. We lose more people to measles than anything else."

"I told the woman that," Tula put in, not looking at Sarah.

During Hauser's gentle pitch, the three of them had wandered into the small church. It smelled of damp earth and decay. In the corner was an ancient piano; the white keys had turned yellow with age. Sarah pushed a key and it made a hollow, tinny sound. "Out of tune," she said with an edge of sadness.

"I'm afraid so."

"It was used for services," Tula explained. "Long ago in the past."

Sarah spotted the hospital sheds and started toward them.

Elliot quickly moved to her side. "Oh, you don't want to go in there. There are other things you'll want to see. The boys' workshop is—"

She cut him off, saying, "If it's the hospital, I'd like to see it."

He stared at her with a mixture of admiration and apprehension. It was clear that he was dealing with a strong willed young woman, who was determined to bear witness at whatever cost to her physical and mental health. Beneath her quiet manner she was strong and tough, and he sensed that she would always find a way to get what she wanted. Graciously, he gestured her on.

The stench of illness, rot, and decay inside the hospital was overpowering, but Sarah fought against an impulse to show any sign of repulsion. She was a part of this world now; she was not a guest. She had to breathe the air that the others breathed and fully accept the reality of this human misery.

She glanced around. The floor beds—cloth mats spread over wood—were jammed with patients as medical orderlies attended to them. Sarah followed Hauser as they walked past distended abdomens, goiterous necks, rash-ravaged skin. She listened in horror to the symphony of moans and cries and strangled weeping. She gagged and quickly caught herself. She said with a nervous glance at Elliot, "I guess it takes some getting used to."

"I'm still not used to it," he assured her, "even after all these years. You'll be fine." But he was worried that maybe she wouldn't be fine. Too much reality too soon and she might tuck in her tail and fly home to London, leaving them high and dry. Leaving them with one less donor.

Sarah was keenly aware that she might be in over her head. She had never been in the trenches. Saving lives was not so much a matter of pretty sentiments as it was just gutting it out day by day. She could see that now, and every nerve in her body was telling her to turn away and run and never look back, telling her to forget that such a world as this existed. But she walked on, past windows open to the brutal heat and the flies. She would not fold. She could not conceive of returning to Henry having lost her nerve.

At the far end of the room they came up behind Callahan and his assistant, Hamadi, a young and clever Ethiopian resident. They were in mid-operation on Gemilla. Callahan looked up, a frown passing across his features, then carried on with the surgery. He was still smarting from their earlier exchange, and, unable to control himself, said without looking up, "Well, if it isn't Mrs. Bauford. Are you enjoying yourself? Are you gathering material for your memoirs?"

"Nick. . . ." Elliot cautioned.

Callahan continued, saying, "You won't see this in medical school, I guarantee you that. Not even on *M*A*S*H*. In fact this makes *M*A*S*H* look like your Columbia-Presbyterian in New York City."

He was right—angry and overbearing as usual, but right. Sarah had never seen sights so crude and gory and appalling. She looked down at the bleeding, semi-anesthetized Gemilla, her swollen body protruding through her robe. Facial twitches rippled across her features, revealing her struggle with the pain.

"Kat," Callahan yelled without looking up. "Front and center."

A tough-looking, muscular white nurse—hard to judge her age, Sarah thought—leaned close to Gemilla and pressed her palm firmly onto an organ in her lower abdomen. Sarah's nostrils flared at the putrid odor that filled the air. Sensing her discomfort, Callahan smiled as he continued to work.

"If you're thinking of throwing up," he said, "don't do it. We have enough problems. Close your eyes and think of ponies and nice expensive dinners and vacation spas and country weekends."

He turned to Sarah with a brief half smile. "Don't look now, Mrs. Bauford, because this is really, *really* disgusting." He carried on snipping and digging, and Sarah forced herself not to look away. There was no way on earth she would let this man defeat her. She would die first.

"The boy," she said, breaking the silence, "Abraha—is he being looked at?"

Callahan glanced up, a strange light in his eyes. She couldn't decipher it: Was he making fun of her or beginning to appraise her from a different angle? "Yes, ma'am," he answered slowly. "He's being checked out now, as you instructed. One shed over."

Sarah looked away, embarrassed by her perceived bossiness. She felt so uncomfortable and defensive around this man and felt constantly compelled to justify herself. He made her feel like a spoiled rich girl, which she definitely was not and never had been. Why couldn't he see her for the person she was?

Suddenly Gemilla reached up and gripped Sarah's hand, her eyes burning into Sarah as she tried to say something. Sarah leaned close to her as the woman repeated again again, "So'a . . . so'a . . . so'a . . . so'a. . . ."

"What is she saying?" Sarah asked Callahan.

"Soda," Callahan answered. He shouted to a black nurse's aid, "Monica, give her your Fanta."

The nurse poured a few drops of Fanta over

her fingers and held her hand to Gemilla's mouth. The dying woman sucked at the soda on the nurse's fingertips.

"God," Sarah said under her breath, twisting her head away.

"Too much for you?" Callahan said.

"I'm okay." She forced herself to look back at Gemilla and the nurse. The only sound was a "smick, smick, smick" as the dying woman sucked the soda.

Callahan said quietly, "You see how it is? We all have our needs and they're always relative. Let's say you own a Bentley. But you aspire to a Rolls-Royce. But this woman's world is a suck of soda. That's all she lives for. Nothing else matters. Weird, isn't it? All those plans you have, places to go, people to meet, exciting things to do . . . and this is what can happen. And it can happen to us all. Where a suck of soda is the only thing that matters in the world. Think about it." He worked in silence, then added, "Humbling, isn't it?"

Monica withdrew her fingers. Gemilla, sated from the few drops of soda she had consumed, leaned back still holding Sarah's hand in a surprisingly tight grip, a series of little moans escaping from her lips.

Sarah said, "She's hurting, doctor. Can't you give her something?"

"Sure. No big thing. Hey, Monica, call down to the pharmacy for more morphine, would you?"

He shook his head and sighed. "Just where the hell do you think we are here—*Saint Elsewhere?*"

Sarah drew in a deep breath. "I don't deserve your sarcasm."

"Well, that's your opinion."

"The woman is in pain. Something has to be done."

Callahan looked up. "You just don't get it, do you? Your friend here is beyond pain. She has entered another realm. It happens all the time."

"Have you asked her that, or is this some medical theory of yours?"

"Ah. So sarcasm cuts both ways." He said to Hamadi, "Ask the patient if it hurts."

The intern, still stitching, muttered in dialect in Gemilla's ear. She answered in a quick burst of gasped syllables. Hamadi, glancing shyly at Sarah, said, "She say she feel pain of hunger. But she know death is even more hungry than pains . . . so she give thanks." He glanced gravely at Callahan and added, "She give thanks to you, Doctor Nick. She call you new name. Kisalu. . . ."

"Kisalu, Kisalu," Gemilla whispered under her breath, giving a slight movement of her head.

"What does that mean?" Sarah asked.

"Kisalu." Hamadi paused, thinking for a moment. "It mean 'he who steals from death.'"

"That is beautiful," she said. She glanced at Callahan, judging his reaction, but he had already moved away from the cot. She suspected that he was a man who avoided anything emotional, no matter how authentic. She watched him as he changed his mask and scrubbed away at his hands in a clean but rusted pot.

There is a softness deep in him, she thought. A whole country of unexplored feeling. I wonder if it's possible for anyone to get close to him. I wonder if anyone has ever had the courage to try.

Later, certain that she was alone, Sarah stood in the abandoned church, wiping roughly at her arms, her dress, her hands—all in one frantic attempt to rid her body of the stench and feel of death. She hated herself for such an obvious show of weakness, but she was in the grip of obsession and fear. She continued to rub as the scenes of disease and death scrolled across her mind. Maybe Henry had been right. Maybe this was all a huge mistake. Was she driven more by her ego than her convictions? Was she, deep down, everything that Nick Callahan seemed to suggest? A spoiled little rich girl? Slowly, as she stood there, she began to get a grip on her emotions. The trembling abated and she took a few deep breaths. She suddenly missed Henry with an aching intensity, missed his arms around her, his sweet attentiveness. She missed his decency, his many small kindnesses to her. She missed his lightness and laughter, their nights out with friends, their lovemaking. . . . She glanced across the room at the piano. She walked over, lifted the lid and sat on a bench as she stared at the brittle, yellowed keys. She banged out some musical phrases, but they were hardly music. "There is no music here," she said out loud. She lowered the lid and rested her head against the warm wood. She felt tears welling up. But she would not allow herself to cry. She was beyond tears, just as Nick Callahan was beyond tears. She was determined to be his equal and to force him to see beneath the surface of her to the depths she knew that she possessed.

In the therapeutic feeding center the next morning, Sarah leaned over a makeshift cot, trying to feed Abraha, coaxing his head from its lifeless slump. His limbs feebly resisted as she tipped the cup of watery cereal to his lips. He coughed it out; she tried again. As she struggled to feed him, she sang softly—and hummed when she couldn't remember the words—the lullabies of her childhood.

Callahan came up behind her and observed her for a moment. His expression was inscrutable.

After a moment he said quietly, "Do you think he's really going to sit up and drink?"

Sarah's head jerked up and she felt the heat of a blush suffuse her face.

"I'm trying to get some nourishment into him. I don't expect miracles, doctor."

Callahan shook his head, and Sarah, reading his eyes, saw something other than the usual impatience and anger—something more akin to pity.

"The child is dying," he said. "He can barely move his lips, let alone drink from a cup."

"I'm sorry. I realize you're the expert, you know what's going to happen. I'm only trying to help."

"Forget it," he said. "You don't know what you're doing."

Sarah felt the sting of his words like a slap in the face. Hot tears of frustration filled her eyes. She watched Callahan turn away abruptly and walk off. Suddenly she jumped to her feet, indignant, overwhelmed, all of her pent-up emotions exploding from within her.

"Who do you think you are?" she said, her voice trembling, on the verge of hysteria. "You stand there with your 'look at me' supercilious grin. I mean, do you really suppose that the only reason I came here was so some smart-ass Brit could shit on me about how I don't know this and don't know that? Of *course* I don't. That's why I'm here—so I can find out. And as for you—Doctor

Callahan—for all I know you're as brilliant at what you do as you seem to think you are, but you're not Jesus Christ. You say the child won't live. *But you don't know that.* I'm sick and tired of men who play God. . . ."

Her outburst was followed by absolute silence. Callahan's eyes widened and she thought he looked stunned. For the first time she could glimpse the boy in him, habitually buried beneath his beard and an imperious attitude.

"Well, I guess I lost it," she said, breaking the silence at last. "But we all have our breaking points, you know."

The silence stretched as Callahan continued to study her. He seemed to be searching for something, and judging from his penetrating stare he might have found it. Sarah sensed that the ground between them had shifted slightly; they were, she felt, in some unspoken sense, more equal than before.

"Am I supposed to accept that as an apology?"

"Not really."

He nodded. "American woman," he said, speaking softly.

"What do you mean by that?"

"You *are* American, aren't you?"

"Yes."

"You speak your mind. You're not afraid."

"Oh, I wouldn't say that, Doctor Callahan. I'm plenty afraid."

Quietly, in a tone still faintly guarded, he said, "Okay—you want to do something? You want to make yourself useful? Get some H.E.M.—that's high-energy milk—Elliot will give it to you. Tease it around the child's mouth with your finger and let him suck at that. Small amounts only. If he revives, call a nurse. If he doesn't, at least he'll have someone with him when he dies."

"He isn't going to die," Sarah said.

A quick look passed between them, full of questions and words unspoken, then Callahan turned away and stomped out of the tent.

Night came on quickly, but the heat remained like an ache that persisted. The sky was immense and black, save for the cluster of stars strung from horizon to horizon. In the burial field Joss Newcombe was overseeing the burial of the day's dead with his local crew. "Let's move along, mates," he said in his hearty voice that belied his troubled and drawn expression. "I'm developing a mighty thirst." Most of his crew understood no English at all and he usually spoke to them in Tigreyan. Sometimes, though, he preferred to use his own language and they responded to his manner and gestures and were quick to follow orders. Chewing on an unlit cigar, Joss made a notation in his small notebook, which he carried in his hip pocket: *43 to be buried today. 17 children, 15 adult males, 11 adult females. Sic transit gloria mundi.*

When the dead were buried, Joss joined Hauser, Callahan, Tula, Kat, Ribs, and Monica at the campfire beyond the abandoned church. They sat around a small fire, sipping beer, slapping at mosquitoes, and discussing the camp situation.

Callahan said, "Ribs? Kat? How many did you lose today?"

"We think eleven from our side."

"Twelve," Monica corrected as Kat looked at her questioningly. "The ten-year-old. She died while you were in the field."

Joss tapped his notebook and said wearily, "I tallied it up. Forty-three today." He tipped up his can of beer and drank deeply.

Callahan stared at the fire and shook his head. "Shit. That's more than yesterday."

"I know," Joss said. "Thirty-five was the count. Twenty-nine the day before that. We're goin' the wrong way, Nick."

Callahan watched Joss closely. The Australian was one of the toughest, most even-tempered men he had ever known, and he had the greatest respect for him. But something wasn't right with him. He hoped Joss wasn't cracking under the strain; the camp couldn't afford to lose him. He would be impossible to replace.

"Maybe tomorrow will be better," Callahan said casually, shooting a look at Newcombe.

The Australian gave a shrug and said nothing.

"For now," he continued, still staring at Joss, "switch more of your full-time crew to the gravesite. We're eating up too much time." He turned to Ribs and said, "Give us a week's worth of holes. Make it a nightshift so nobody sees you working. Can't have people dying of depression, eh?"

"The woman," Tula said. "We protect her. . . ." She quickly raised a finger to her lips. "Shh. She be here."

In the shadows outside the circle, Sarah stepped shyly up. Seeing her hover uncertainly, Hauser smiled and beckoned to her to sit beside him. Callahan glanced at her and nodded silently.

"You like a beer, Mrs. Bauford?" Joss asked.

"Yes, thank you."

Callahan said, "Joss, what's the water situation?"

"Fuck all awful," he answered, shooting an apologetic look and a shrug toward Sarah. "The new well came up dry. Crankshaft's bust to buggery and we're down to two liters per person per day." He hesitated, then added, "That explains why the count's going up."

"Why didn't you tell me this earlier?"

"Didn't want to ruin your day, mate."

"Well, you've sure as hell ruined my evening."

There was a murmur of laughter. Gallows humor was appreciated in the refugee camp; for a few moments it could drive away the specter of death.

"What about the tankers?" Elliot asked.

Joss, busily lighting the stump of a cigar, looked up. "Sure, they'll do fine for a few days, but basically if we don't get the well up and running, we're fucked. We won't be operational. Everybody dies."

"So," Elliot said, "what do you need exactly?"

"Christ, mate, I just told you. A new crankshaft."

Everyone looked at Joss, surprised by his anger. He was ordinarily the most jovial and amiable of men.

The death count is getting to him, Callahan thought grimly. He's burying too many bodies.

"Okay, fine," Elliot said softly, trying to diffuse the situation. "We'll see what we can do."

"Yeah." Joss extended the word out to absurdity, clearly unconvinced. "Better snap to it. We're talking hours here."

The group fell into an uncomfortable silence. Callahan shot a quick look at Sarah, who returned his stare. He quickly looked away.

"Well," Elliot said, "the good news is, the government's coming. . . ."

"Ah Christ, not again," Callahan said as the others moaned.

"Yessir," Elliot continued. "Mister Ningpopo himself, the pedant of poverty, the master of his mean little universe. Ours for about one hour, if we're lucky. . . ."

"That long, Elliot?" Monica said with a wry smile. "It's awfully generous of Mister Ningpopo. How did we get so lucky?"

The others laughed.

"Well put, Monica," Elliot said. "So let's be ready for the tiny tyrant. Each of you talk to me and we'll get our requests squared away."

"Two hookers and a single to Melbourne," Joss said. This brought snickers followed by an uneasy pause. The Australian's dark humor fit the general mood—flat, weary, discouraged, in need of a general lift. Callahan studied the others, gauging their general mood. What he saw worried him. When he spoke it was quietly, from the heart and as much for his own benefit as for theirs. He was more instinctively than self-consciously the leader, which was not his usual style.

"First thing Nincompoop will do is study his list after Elliot tells him what we need. He'll look up all serious and important and say, 'This item not on list. You cannot have.'" His imitation of the bureaucrat was uncanny and the others burst into spontaneous laughter. He let the moment linger and then said, "Seriously, folks, here's what we're going to do. First thing in the morning, Kat, Monica, and anyone else with a needle, we start immunizing all the children against measles, youngest first, then up the line till we run out, okay? That way we can honestly tell Nincompoop, no medicine. Get it to us fast, man. Then . . . sanitation . . . Joss, Ribs—you need to cut a defecation field somewhere beyond the camp until the well's fixed. We should chlorinate all the water."

Elliot said, "Not the tanker water, Nick. The tanker water's—"

"Fuck the tanker water," Callahan cut in. "Who says the bloody stuff has to taste good? Just chlorinate the whole lot. There's too much infection to risk leaving it alone. There'll be no raging plagues on my watch, if I can help it."

He scowled at Hauser, who shrugged and said, "Right, Nick. That's what we'll do then."

"Good," Callahan said, rising and stretching. He grinned. "A big day ahead of us tomorrow. Let's rock 'n' roll, people."

They applauded Callahan ironically, sprinkling in some jeers and catcalls, and he gave a deep bow, also ironically.

Sarah realized for the first time that these people were a family. They bickered, they disagreed, they compromised, they laughed together, they suffered together. She watched Callahan closely, impressed by the way he smiled at them with affection. It was plain that he loved them and that they loved him in return. He had managed to lift their mood by being the spiritual father they so obviously needed. It was equally plain that she was the outsider.

The party broke up and people began to drift off to their beds.

Elliot smiled at Sarah and said, "Good night, Mrs. Bauford."

"Good night, Elliot." She hesitated, then added, "Would you mind calling me Sarah?"

"Not at all. I'd be happy to."

"You see, I think of Mrs. Bauford as my mother-in-law. It just doesn't fit me—not yet anyway."

"I understand." He noticed a tension in her features, a tightness around the eyes that hadn't been there when she had first arrived at camp. "Are you doing okay?" he said.

She smiled. "I'm doing okay."

"It's rough out here. It takes some getting used to."

"I'll do fine. Please don't worry about me."

"I promise that I won't. Good night, Sarah."

"Good night."

Callahan headed toward Hauser, who had stopped to talk to one of the native workers. He was fluent in Tigreyan—unlike Joss who spoke the language in the most functional sense: simple commands and exhortations and jokes—and the locals loved him for his ability to communicate with them. On his way past Sarah, Callahan paused and sniffed the air.

"What is that?" he said. "That smell . . . is that perfume? Are you wearing perfume in the middle of the desert?" He shook his head and widened his eyes comically as though in a state of stupefaction. "What in the world will you think of next?"

Sarah blushed as Callahan began chuckling in gentle disbelief. But for the first time his attitude was neither malign nor challenging, and she found herself laughing, too.

"Good night, Mrs. Bauford."

"Good night, Doctor Callahan."

He started to walk away, but then turned back. "Oh, I forgot," he said. "Your friend—the boy's mother. She died this afternoon."

Gemilla . . . Gemilla is gone. Now Abraha has no one. Sarah stared at Callahan's retreating back. She felt utterly lost, as lonely as the desert that surrounded her. *The woman suffered so much and now she is gone.* Tears filled Sarah's eyes as she stumbled blindly toward her sleeping quarters.

Elliot shot Callahan an angry glance. Anger was foreign to his nature and the doctor was on his guard.

"Tell me something, Nick. Do you do that on purpose? Are you deliberately setting out to hurt that woman?"

"I don't know what you mean."

"Yes, you know, dammit. And it's wrong. Stop it. Stop being an asshole. I mean it, Nick—cease and desist. She's generous and we need her. Stop alienating her."

Callahan nodded, looking almost sheepish. Elliot Hauser was the only person whom he could call a true friend, and the only one who could talk to him like a brother or a father and get away with it. To most of the camp Callahan was the leader and the father figure, but to Elliot he was the unruly brother who often needed lessons in discipline and comportment. They had been the closest of friends for years, partly because Callahan could not bluff and bully Elliot into letting him have his way.

The two men walked to their quarters in silence. Callahan did not apologize for his behavior—he never could bring himself to do that—but Hauser could tell that he was penitent.

He said, "I think if we're lucky we might hold out five, maybe six more days. That is, if we're lucky."

Callahan nodded, his head sunk toward his chest in thought. There was no banter now. No effort to rally his friend. The nature of their friendship was such that they never lied to each other, or pretended.

"What about your old man?" Callahan said. "The trust fund. Anything there?"

"Are you kidding? My father was the politest 'fuck you' we got in our last solicitation."

"I didn't realize that. You never told me."

"That's because I don't bother you with the details—not till I have to. Your job is to save lives. Mine is to save us—keep us afloat."

"Who has the harder job, El?"

"You do, my friend. By light-years."

With an embarrassed grin, Callahan said, "Listen—you know sometimes I'm a bit of a shit." He shrugged. "You know that, right?" It was the closest he could come to an apology.

"Fucking outrageous is what you are," Elliot said, laughing. "Yes, I'm painfully aware of your many shortcomings. But if you weren't a handful, you wouldn't be Nick Callahan. I guess we have to take the dross with the gold."

"So . . ." Callahan surveyed the darkening camp, silent now in uneasy slumber.

"So," Elliot said. "It looks like it's over unless Ningpopo comes through for us. We tried, Nick. God knows, no one has ever tried harder."

Callahan said, "What about Steiger?"

Elliot gave him a hard look, frowning and troubled. "Come on, man. You've got to be kidding."

"It might be our only option. Some small favors. A little information on the rebels—"

"Stash a shit load of weapons," Elliot put in. "And that's just for starters. Nick, you've got no idea. I'm afraid you're a bit naïve in this area. I don't think you understand the games these people play."

"So what if he's fucking over the Marxists? What's that got to do with us? They all play their ridiculous politics while we try to save lives. Saving lives is what it's all about. And by the way—what have the Marxists done for us lately?"

"We don't swim in those waters, Nick. They're shark infested."

"But it's in a good cause, man, and what's more important than that? And frankly, Steiger is all we've got."

"I told you, it's out of the question."

"Why, for Christ's sake? Give me reasons that make sense in the real world. We've got thousands of people fucking dying on us here. What does Marxism and the CIA and all the rest of those shit bags mean to them? They want to eat, Elliot, and that's not the bottom line, it's the only line. They eat or they die. End of story."

Hauser turned to his friend and took his arm in a tight grip. He stared into his eyes and said, "Because that's not the way we started. We play into Steiger's hands and all the rest of them and we're soiled. Mission totally fucked up. The ends do not justify the means."

"This isn't philosophy hour," Callahan said. "I'm not sure you're right—not when I stand out here in the night and smell the stench of death. This is no time to be precious."

There was a tense silence. The two men stood inches from each other, their eyes engaged in a battle.

"Sorry," Elliot said at last. "I won't go there. If you decide to, you do it without me. We started clean and I say we stay clean. You may consider it naïve and silly, but I have to live with my conscience.

I can't conceive of operating any other way."

Callahan glared at his friend, neither of them willing to give an inch. Then very faintly, on the thinnest edge of audibility, came the sound of a piano. It was out of tune and the sound was hollow, but anyone listening closely, and possessing any musical knowledge, would have known that the keys were struck with authority.

They both were silent, listening intently.

"What is that?" Nick said.

"Schumann, I think," Elliot replied.

"I didn't know the piano worked."

"It doesn't. Somebody must be using magic."

The melody of "Dreaming" from Schumann's *Scenes from Childhood* floated out softly over the African night, momentarily bathing the vast camp of refugees in a tableau of landscape and man unified and at peace.

Callahan said a hurried goodnight to Hauser and walked to the canvas arch of the entrance to the abandoned church. He quietly ducked inside and watched Sarah play. He had known it was her playing. From the first note struck he had seen her face, had seen her sitting at the piano. She was bent over the brittle yellowed keys playing simply and with great feeling, her only light the dim hurricane lamp perched on a crate beside the piano. He drank from the bottle of beer he had carried from the campfire, soaking in the sweet anomaly of this music in this place.

Sarah paused to twist a pink hair band in two and wrapped her long dark locks into a ponytail. The task complete, she settled her fingers softly on the keys again and resumed where she had left off. But she stopped almost immediately, sensing that she was being watched. She turned and searched the darkness; there was no one there. After a momentary pause, she turned back to the piano and finished the piece.

Later still, approaching midnight, Sarah, unable to sleep, knelt over a bucket sponging her arms and face. In a shard of mirror she inspected the ring of dirt that smudged her face and neck. Honest filth, she thought. I've earned this. She cupped more water in her hand and continued washing. Sounds outside—the snapping of a twig, the sifting of dry dirt—froze her in mid-movement. Her muscles tensed. She followed a shadow as it crossed the fabric of the tent. She watched as it circled slowly.

Callahan appeared at the opening to the tent.

"I dream of childhood," he said. "I dream of love. Of a garden where a boy plays, forever young . . ."

"You heard me playing."

"Themes from Childhood," he said. "Part of a series from Schumann's lederhosen. One of my favorites."

Sarah smiled. "Lederhosen are trousers, Doctor Callahan."

Slowly he returned her smile. "Ah."

"The German for 'song' is lieder."

"Lieder," he repeated. "Yes. Correct. I was amazed to hear music coming from the church. I didn't think the piano worked."

"It doesn't really. I just willed a few notes from it."

"Magic," he mumbled.

"What did you say?"

"Nothing."

She was still kneeling over the bucket and Callahan watched her intently. After a moment she stood and toweled her face dry.

"I'm sorry. . . . is there something I can do?"

"No," he answered quickly. "I saw the light as I passed and thought I'd better check."

"I'm fine. Just having trouble sleeping."

"This place isn't conducive to sleep. I exist on about three hours' sleep a night." He fumbled for something else to say, for an adequate reason that brought him to her tent in the middle of the night. He could think of nothing.

"Well, I'm glad you stopped by."

"The baby," he said after another pause. "Did you try the H.E.M.?"

"Yes."

"And?"

"No change, I'm afraid."

"It may take a while. He's very sick, you know."

"I know."

Callahan coughed nervously, and, looking away, said, "I'm sorry about your friend—the boy's mother. I'm sometimes rather brusque."

"I've noticed that," she said with a smile. "I accept your apology, Doctor Callahan."

"Everyone calls me Nick," he said. "Even little children."

"Okay, Nick. And little children call me Sarah."

He grinned, took a sip of beer, then said. "See you in the morning," and faded into the darkness—gone as silently as he had come.

6

Dawn came and the death count continued to rise. As the sun filled the sky,
bloody and huge on the eastern horizon,
Joss and the local crew of twenty workers were
busy burying nearly seventy bodies, all wrapped in
white winding sheets—the bodies of those who
had died during the night. Joss was unusually
silent, not joking with his crew and exhorting
them on in his usual fashion. His face was set in
grim lines. He picked up a body, passed it to one
of his crew, then, without a word of warning, he
left the work party.

Half an hour later, Callahan found him sitting
on a rock in the desert, about a mile from camp.
The sun was burning in the sky, and he was bare-

headed, oblivious to the heat, holding in his hand an empty bottle of beer.

Callahan regarded him solemnly. "Joss?"

"Yeah. One and the same."

"Is this what you call a walkabout, mate?"

"I reckon so," he said flatly. "Call it what you want." He sighed, his eyes fixed on the vast, belittling horizon, shimmering with mirages that seemed to have no end.

"What's wrong, Joss?"

The Australian squinted up at him. "Wrong question. What isn't wrong is the heart of the matter."

"Okay. Let's go with that." Callahan squatted on his haunches with a groan and let the silence stretch until Joss said, "Why don't they just get it over with, eh? Why don't they all just die? It's why they're here, isn't it? It's sure as hell why I'm here. I'm the guy who buries the dead."

"Joss," Callahan said softly. "Don't go south on me, man. I need you."

"I mean," Joss said, following his thought, "if they'd just get on with it and die, then I can dig *one big fucking hole and end it.*"

Callahan rested a hand on the Australian's shoulder, watching the big man's face slowly crumple. He turned away from Callahan and his back arched with the tears that he could no longer hide.

Minutes passed until Callahan said finally, "You

don't like what you see? You think it's too harsh?"

"Leave me alone. Maybe you should butt out, mate."

"Do you want me to milk it down a bit? Make things a little less real?"

"Shut up!"

"Look into their eyes," Callahan said. "Don't look away—you've got to look *in*. The first thing you see is the utter reality—call it hunger, call it need, call it desperation, it's beyond words to describe it—it's the only thing that cuts through this bullshit. Because if there's one thing I've learned—one really important lesson—it's that you can't protect yourself from suffering. Only when you're really lonely, really shit-scared, do you get even *close* to what these people endure." He squeezed the Australian's shoulder. "This is it, mate. Bottom line. It doesn't get any more real than this."

Joss looked up and stared at him. His eyes were swollen and inflamed, but dry.

"I lost it," he said.

"We all lose it. It comes with the territory."

Joss rose slowly from the rock.

"I'd better get back," he said. "There's nothing worse than an idle crew." A slow grin creased his weathered face. "Right, mate?"

Later that morning, Callahan sat at the immunization table organizing the long lines of refugees and checking remaining vaccines against the number of patients. When he felt that the line was moving too slowly he clapped his hands and shooed everyone along, helping one woman as she struggled with her two infants, speaking soothingly to the fearful who shrank back, urging them to approach the table.

He turned to Tula who was working beside him, busily administering vaccines and chatting away merrily with the women and children. The men she mostly ignored.

"How are we doing?" he said.

"Okay, Doctor Nick. But not much left."

Callahan glanced at the line, counting under his breath. "There may just be enough."

Kat shook her head. "No, Nick. We're going to run out."

"Well, there's enough for the kids," he said sharply. "That's all we can do right now. So there's enough—right, Kat?"

She shrugged and rolled her eyes. "Sure—if you say so."

"I do," he said with a grin. He quickly moved along the line, cajoling, soothing, playing the doctor man to the hilt. At the tent flap, he stared out. In the distance, crossing the square in the shimmering heat, he watched as Sarah entered the therapeutic feeding center. His eyes lingered after she had disappeared inside. She's a brave woman, he thought. I'll give her that. Brave and stubborn as hell. All the days and nights she's spent trying to keep that child alive. You've got to hand her that. But if that child doesn't live . . . He shook his head, not wanting to complete the thought.

Sarah spent the afternoon with Abraha, and after a quick bite of dinner she returned to him. She crooned to him, she held him in her arms, on her left breast so that he could feel the beating of her heart. He needed to be a part of her; she was certain that their physical closeness would help to pull him through this terrible ordeal. The child remained pitifully weak, sucking what he could from her finger in tiny, desperate intakes of breath. His eyes moved slowly, unseeingly; the boy was barely alive. Two or three times during that endless day she feared that she had lost him, but each time he rallied and moved away from the edge of eternity. She bent to her task hour after hour, fiercely focused, her will like iron. She would not allow him to give up; she could not.

Elliot Hauser, making his afternoon rounds, came up behind her and watched her for a moment, unseen.

"Sarah," he said after a moment.

She turned, her eyes glazed with tiredness. "Hi, Elliot."

"You need some sleep."

"I hate to leave him, even for a moment. I'm afraid if I do . . ." Her voice trailed off.

"You're doing everything humanly possible. But you mustn't neglect yourself. That won't do him any good."

"I sometimes wonder if he even knows I'm here. It's been two weeks. I'm not sure there's any improvement."

"He knows you're here," Elliot said with a shake of his head. "Some part of him knows. And that means more than you can imagine."

"Do you really think so?"

He nodded.

His gentle encouragement was almost too much for her to bear. She did not feel deserving; she felt confused and lost. She forced a smile as tears blurred her eyes.

"Thanks, Elliot."

"For what? What have I done?"

"Just for being you."

He glanced away, embarrassed by her show of feeling.

"Good night, Sarah," he said. "Keep up the good work."

"Good night," she said.

She collapsed into her tent after midnight, suffering from a wracking headache, and almost immediately fell into a dark and bottomless nightmare. Abraha's face dissolved and then metamorphosed into a series of grotesque images—bloated and disease-ravaged—which Sarah had witnessed over the past days. Abraha became all of those goitered necks, those pus-filled, running sores, those fly-coated, skeletal bodies, he became Gemilla's sucking mouth.

She awoke screaming. She sat on the edge of the cot, wide-awake, terrified, panting. Her body dripped with sweat. Faintly, as she sat there trying to gather herself, she heard the sound of a child crying from the direction of the feeding tent. She held her breath and listened. The crying grew louder. She stiffened. "Abraha," she muttered to herself. *"Is that Abraha?"* Confused and panicked, she grabbed the bucket of H.E.M. and rushed out into the night toward the tent where the child lay.

As she entered the tent, the crying suddenly stopped. She saw that Tula was leaning over the child, adjusting the blankets, soothing him with soft words.

Tula looked up and regarded her, a strange light in her eyes. "If a child cry," she said, "that is good. Strong enough to scream. When a child is weak . . ." She pressed a finger lightly to her lips. "No good. Just die." A flicker of a smile passed her lips. "This is good. Doctor Nick say he may have passed the crisis." She rose from the edge of the cot. "The child want you. He is awake enough now to know the difference. He cry for you."

"Thank you, Tula."

"I do nothing."

For a moment the two women shared a look

that for the first time bound them together: a look of respect.

"He is your child," Tula said quietly before disappearing into the night. Sarah sat beside Abraha softly caressing his cheeks—no longer feverish—running a hand over his tightly matted hair.

"You're going to make it," she chanted. "You're going to make it, Abraha. You're going to make it. You're going to make it. . . ."

Early in the morning Sarah was washing herself in yesterday's basin water, now the color of slate, when Tula rushed into the tent, breathless.

"Baby woman," she said, "come! Come quick!"

Not bothering to dry herself, Sarah jogged across the camp after Tula to the therapeutic feeding center. She raced inside and pulled up short. Callahan was bent over the cot checking the child. He gently placed Abraha in a cradle attached to a scale. He rested his stethoscope across the boy's abdomen, then slid it slowly up to the heart, listening intently, then moved the stethoscope again, covering the child's entire chest. Abraha was showing visible signs of life—tiny fists clenching and unclenching, his eyes open and no longer milky with illness.

Sarah stared in wonder. Then she turned to Callahan and met his gaze.

He nodded. "Yes," he said. "One life . . ."

On his face was the faintest trace of a smile.

"You can hold him. I think he's waiting for your arms."

Without a word, Sarah picked up the child and held him close to her heart.

Callahan watched the woman and the African child, so bound together at this moment, and then reached into his pocket and withdrew a pink hair band.

"I found this outside your tent," he said. "Late last night. It's yours, isn't it?"

"Yes."

He placed it on a chair beside the cot.

She gently rocked the child, her eyes dreamy, far away. Callahan had seen that look in the eyes of women who had just given birth.

He stood indecisively, watching her, and at that moment Elliot Hauser popped his head into the tent.

"Ningpopo has just arrived," he said.

The Ethiopian government convoy, comprised of two vans and soldiers in two jeeps mounted with machine guns, had arrived in a cloud of yellow dust. The chief government administrator of the region, Dawit Ningpopo, stepped down. He was a diminutive, Napoleonic-like man from Addis Ababa, dressed in a charcoal gray, double-breasted suit showing a white collar and cuffs. An assistant followed directly behind him, not unlike a human shadow, anticipating his every need.

Ningpopo was the survivor of many purges and tribal wars. He was a politician, adept and chameleonlike in his ability to assume the positions and prejudices of whichever party happened to be in power at the moment. He was utterly loyal to those who held that power and he was ruthless in demanding that same degree of fealty from those beneath him. Like many small men, Ningpopo possessed an ego that was swollen beyond measure and he aspired to great heights, which he was shrewd enough to realize would only be achieved in his imagination.

Ningpopo sat in the one comfortable chair in Elliot's office, one small leg crossed over the other, and affected a thoughtful frown as he listened to Elliot. Callahan, Sarah and several others had crowded into the room. Paperwork lay strewn about. Both the copy and fax machines were working, and a scum of dust and humidity covered all the surfaces.

"Today," Elliot said, "we hit eight hundred calories. We estimate we'll be down to five hundred in a few days. Maybe even less than that. Bottom line—we're not going to make next week's distribution."

"Not a chance in hell," Callahan put in. "We'll be out of business."

Hauser shot Callahan a warning glance, which said as loud as any words: Let me handle this.

Ningpopo, elaborately ignoring Callahan's interruption, listened to Hauser's pitch with a thoughtful, furrowed brow. In his small, well-manicured hand he held a bright pink plastic fan. It purred, very close to his face, and he shifted its position constantly in a kind of shaving motion.

Elliot spoke slowly and without undue emphasis. "Food is clearly a major issue, but far from the only one. In fact, we do have a problem with security. You see, we're effectively hostages here. Unless these people get more food, I'm not sure I can guarantee the safety of my staff." Elliot attempted a smile. "I'm sure you're aware, Mr. Ningpopo, that a starving man is a most dangerous man."

The official glanced at his notes, which lay spread neatly on his lap. He frowned heavily, looking more and more like an outsized prune. He said, "Food? Security? These are, I believe, listed as separate issues."

Avoiding Callahan's angry glare, Elliot said, "Yes . . . but I'm sure you'd agree they are linked."

Ningpopo scowled, the mini-fan performing a confined arc of nervous movements.

"We cannot control thousands of starving people on promises alone," Elliot continued. "Surely you must realize that. These refugees have nothing to lose. They've already lost everything. They would kill for a crust of bread and trade all the diamonds in Africa for a decent meal." Elliot spread his arms—a sad and fatalistic gesture. "That's the situation. Our backs are to the wall."

"You speak poetically, Mr. Hauser," Ningpopo said. "I deal with facts and figures. They are what interest me."

Elliot nodded and smiled pleasantly, intent on continuing to dance for the Napoleonic Ningpopo. "Okay . . . good. So what do we need? Well, if we could get emergency corn that would be a start."

"I will raise it with the W.F.P.," Ningpopo said.

"Thank you."

The official fingered his notes impatiently. "I will *raise* the issue," he said, "but keep in mind that we are stretched thin."

Callahan cut in, his voice drawn tight with contempt. He said, "They owe us since August anyway. We haven't heard a damn thing. Are they sleeping at the controls—or are they waiting for something?" He rubbed his thumb and first finger together, glaring at Ningpopo and giving him a slow wink.

Ningpopo squinted at Callahan, his brow wrinkled with surprise as though he was just now aware of his presence. "Excuse me?"

"Any emergency corn would be gratefully appreciated," Elliot said, shaking his head at Callahan.

Ningpopo continued to stare at the doctor. A tiny twitch of nerves rippled along his jawbone. "Who owes you, please, pardon me. . . ."

"The W.F.P.," Callahan answered. "Three months' worth of corn. It's there in your notes. Take a look."

Ningpopo continued to regard Callahan, never

once blinking. The two men were caught in a staring contest, neither one willing to be the first to look away.

"My notes make no mention of the W.F.P., sir. You are mistaken."

"Then your notes are wrong, Mr. Ningpopo."

Elliot quickly cut in. "If we could address the issue of security for a moment. There is a very real and present danger that—"

Ningpopo shook his fan violently and interrupted, saying, "Our soldiers have no experience of this order, Mr. Hauser. However, this is an area that can be examined and we can provide you with subsequent information."

Ningpopo's assistant, after a quick glance at his watch, leaned forward and whispered in his ear. The official nodded gravely and said, "In fact we have another meeting at the Korem camp at noon. Now. Please. We will discuss these issues separately in the proper order, please, pardon me." A delicate flourish of his fan, then: "It does no good to jump around from food to security and to wherever your concerns may take you. It is simply not coherent. Decisions cannot be made in such a context of confusion."

Callahan's voice rose. "Not coherent. *Not coherent?*"

"Nick—please," Elliot put in.

Callahan pounded on the desk with the flat of his hand. "If we don't have enough food, these people get hungry. If they get real hungry, if they fucking starve, they start dying. And the hungry ones that don't die, they wreck the camp. Yessir, the issues are linked. You bet they are."

Ningpopo's fan paused in mid-motion.

"Do not raise your voice with me, sir."

Elliot whispered to his friend, "Nick—come on. Let's remain calm. I can handle this."

But Callahan's anger was boiling over now; he was overwhelmed by the woeful conditions in the camp, the bureaucratic stalling, Ningpopo's insufferable arrogance, and Elliot's weakness—he was always so willing to capitulate and expose his jugular to these assholes, getting nothing in return. His face flushed, he said, "Evidently you *can't* handle this, Elliot."

Sarah, watching helplessly as Callahan lashed out at Elliot, put a hand on his arm and said, "Nick—"

"You stay out of this. This is none of your business." He wagged a finger at Ningpopo and continued, saying, "For Christ's sake, Dawit, stop talking bullocks and start getting food delivered— *now*. No fucking excuses, man, no money changing hands. No hanky-panky. Just do it. People are dying here. We're losing forty folks a day on average and that number is on the rise." He took a deep breath. "We are in grave danger of losing the entire camp."

For a moment the room was quiet. Ningpopo's

fan was still. With a faint grunt of discomfort, he rose to his feet.

"Doctor Callahan, sir, your innuendos are most disturbing, pardon me. We do not spend or receive a dollar without accountability. Procedure is a matter of the utmost scrutiny. I assure you that—"

"Procedure my arse," Callahan cut in. "Come on, Dawit, we're not children here. Let's put our cards on the table. You have friends in the water-trucking business whose sole aim in life is to hike up the price by restricting delivery. The old supply and demand con game." Callahan clicked his tongue in disgust. "Are you seriously telling me those shit-ants are following procedure? I'm frankly insulted that you think I'm that stupid and naïve."

Ningpopo's body was beginning to vibrate.

"That is an outrageous accusation, sir, with absolutely no foundation in fact. And coming from you of all people."

"What do you mean by that?" Callahan shouted, pounding the table again.

Ningpopo sneered. His fan was once more working furiously, and his free hand rested on his cocked hip, giving him the look of a nineteenth-century dandy.

"What do I mean, Doctor Callahan? You have committed the most grievous of sins. Taking a young refugee boy from the camp without authorization . . . To die. Yes! To die like some animal in a country he does not even know, far from his own people." Ningpopo spit out the words. "A young, uneducated black boy, used by you for your own strategies. But of course he *was* a black boy, and one more dead African—what would that mean to the world? More specifically, what would it mean to you?"

Callahan exploded from his chair. "Fuck you, Napoleon. I'm warning you, don't say another word."

Elliot grabbed Callahan's arm. "Nick—Jesus—drop it now. We've got to get back on track."

But Callahan shook him off, his inflamed eyes drilling holes in the little African. He couldn't bear to think of JoJo, a boy he had taken under his wing and practically adopted. His dreams were haunted by images of the boy, but that this pestilent bureaucrat, this crook, this fraud, would dare to throw JoJo in his face . . .

Ningpopo, standing straight, unafraid of the bigger man's wrath, refused to back away. He said, "The death of a child in such circumstances is not a minor violation in our country, sir. I can assure you, you are under serious investigation."

"Mr. Ningpopo," Elliot interposed, "it is unnecessary for us to go off on these tangents."

Before he could finish, Callahan leaped forward, trying to reach the official. The room was suddenly a chaos of noise and movement. Two assistants pinned Callahan by the shoulders, Elliot tried to pry them off, and Sarah retreated to the tent flap, fighting a rising tide of hysteria.

He's done it again, she thought. Just like at the Ball. He's shot himself in the foot. Is he trying to destroy himself?

She sensed Ningpopo's eyes on her. She looked up. He was brandishing his fan and the smile he flashed at her made her blood run cold.

8

Ningpopo's convoy disappeared from the camp in a sprawl of dust. His van, cranked up on its back wheels, was being towed by one of the jeeps, and sitting majestically in the rear as though nothing were amiss was Ningpopo, his fan moving furiously across his face. He stared straight ahead and did not acknowledge Elliot's good-bye.

Elliot watched the convoy recede until it dissolved into the grays and tans of the desert, his mouth an angry snip of wire.

"Well, so much for that," he said.

Callahan glanced at him, his expression sheepish. "What?"

"You know damn good and well what I mean.

You blew it, Nick. You blew it big time. You and your ridiculous temper. It's time you learned to live in the real world. You need a course in anger management."

"He wasn't going to do anything, anyway."

"Well, he sure as hell won't now," Elliot snapped.

"The man is totally corrupt."

"But he's the man we have to deal with. Why can't you see that?"

"He had no business bringing up JoJo."

"I agree. That was a low blow," Elliot acknowledged, his tone slightly softer. It was not in his nature to hold a grudge for long. He knew his friend's weaknesses, but respected and admired his many strengths, which were, on balance, far greater.

"I wonder what happened to his car," Elliot said.

"I don't know," Callahan replied, "but I have a sneaking suspicion." He looked around inquiringly. Joss and Ribs were staring at him, big grins on their faces. Tula, Monica, and Kat stood nearby, already in on the joke.

"Joss," Elliot said, "what the hell did you do?"

"I used a wrench, mate. Simple as one, two, three. Ribs, he kept watch. Easy job—ten minutes, tops." And from behind his back, he brought forth a crankshaft.

"Will that fit the well-head?" Elliot asked.

Joss grinned. "Do kangaroos shit in the bush?"

"Good man," Callahan said. "Were you aware that you chose Ningpopo's vehicle?"

"Didn't have a clue. Just took the first one at hand."

His mood fully restored, Callahan roared with laughter. "God must be on our side for a change," he said.

Gradually the camp personnel began heading back to work. Finally only Callahan and Hauser were left in the empty square.

"So I screwed up, eh?" Callahan said softly.

"Yeah, you screwed up," Elliot replied. "Ningpopo is a hateful and disgusting piece of work, I grant you that, but I wish you'd left him to me. Diplomacy isn't your strong suit, Nick."

Callahan nodded. "No place for me in politics, I guess."

"Not a chance."

"Well, it seems we've got no choice now, El. Ningpopo is going to fuck us every which way—which, by the way, I think he would have done anyway. We need Steiger now. It's either him or the end of the line."

The two men stared at each other, but no more was said. No more was necessary.

That night, following the campfire hour, which had begun in high spirits with Joss's retelling of the crankshaft tale and had gradually receded into solemn silence as they all realized how close they were to the camp's total collapse, Sarah crossed the compound. In her hand were traveler's checks. She was headed toward Callahan's tent. Her feelings toward him were in turmoil. His temperamental outbursts frightened her and she despised the condescension she felt he sometimes aimed at her. But she believed in his cause, and for the most part she believed in him. Since childhood—a lonely time spent more with books than friends—she had fantasized about the plight of the underdog and the role she might some day play in righting society's wrongs. She had believed in Robin Hood, one of her earliest fictional heroes. Robbing from the rich to give to the poor struck her as a fair and even beautiful concept. Sarah felt that Nick Callahan, with all of his human flaws, embodied the best traits of Robin Hood: He gave no quarter to the rich and powerful, and something deep inside of her thrilled to his passion.

She walked up to the tent and called out softly, "Nick?"

Hearing no answer, she stepped inside. She looked around before placing the traveler's checks on his cot, curious about his private world. As she turned, her hand flew to her mouth in her nervousness. Callahan was standing in the opening watching her.

She said shyly, "I hope you don't think I'm snooping."

"I'm sure you're not."

"I . . . these are just some traveler's checks. I thought maybe . . . I don't need them. I'm aware how tough things are right now."

"Thanks," he said, unable to hide his surprise. "We are rather back on our heels."

There was an embarrassed pause. Sarah picked up the checks and handed them to him. He stared at the money and then at her.

"Why didn't you give these to Elliot?" he said.

"I don't know," she answered. "It just didn't occur to me."

"He usually handles the money."

"If you prefer, I'll take them to him." She tried to control a flicker of irritation, or disappointment. Nothing she did seemed to make a dent in this man.

"It's okay," he said. "I'll take care of it."

"Thanks."

There was another, longer pause, both of them standing a few feet apart not knowing what to say or quite how to act.

"So," Sarah said, "do you think they'll close you down?"

"It doesn't look good."

"I've gathered that."

"But, you know, if we fail here we always pop up again . . . somewhere. The world is full of the helpless and the destitute." He grinned. "The rich see to that, don't they?"

She did not return his smile but said softly, "This is a little hard to say, but I'm going to say it anyway. I admire you for doing this work."

Callahan shook his head back and forth. "God—that is so American."

She saw color rise in his cheeks; she wondered if he could possibly be blushing.

"Excuse me?"

"You 'admire' me? Why would anyone 'admire' me? What does that mean—'admire'?"

She looked him straight in the eye, trying to control her growing impatience with him. Was he being deliberately obtuse? Was it an act to put her down? It was hard to know with him, given his complex and contradictory nature.

"It means I think what you do is good. It means you do the tough things while others look the other way. It doesn't mean that I like your attitude."

Callahan smiled, more at ease now. He felt comfortable when the situation took on a combative edge.

"Tell me something," he said. "Are you always this difficult?"

"Are you?" she retorted.

"I try to be."

"That's obvious. And practice makes perfect. You succeed at it beautifully."

They fell into silence again while Callahan regarded her. His look was thoughtful, but far from agitated.

"Why don't you ever use my name?" she said, breaking the silence. "In case you've forgotten, it's Sarah."

"I know your name."

"Why don't you ever use it? It's like I somehow don't exist as a person."

"You know whether you do or not. I can't help you there." He sat on the edge of his cot and gestured toward his only chair—a folding canvas beach chair frayed at the edges. "Take a seat."

"I'd prefer to stand, thank you."

Callahan gave a shrug, then said suddenly, "You ever had a cold?"

"A cold? Why sure."

"What's the first thing you do?"

"Chicken soup," she answered. "A dose of NyQuil. Glass of scotch."

"Um hum," he said. "Have you ever just had a cold?"

"I don't follow you."

"You know—you're sick as a dog, can't breathe, coughing your lungs out. And you take nothing. You just have the cold. Ever done that?"

"No."

"No? Of *course* you haven't. That's us, right? We drown it, numb it, kill it . . . anything not to feel. Never just the cold." He cupped his hands around a match against a nonexistent wind and lit a cigarette, then continued, saying, "It's so curious when I think about it. All the time I was a doctor in London no one ever said 'Kisalu' to me. They don't thank you like they thank you here. In this godforsaken place they thank you from their heart, their souls. Because here they feel everything—you understand what I mean? Straight from God. There's no drugs, no painkillers, no chicken soup love for these folks. It's the purest, weirdest thing, suffering. And when you've seen it—when you've seen that kind of courage in a child—how could you ever want to do anything but take him in your arms and hug him to death. Smother him. Protect him."

Callahan dragged deeply on his cigarette, his eyes closed. When he continued, his voice was softer, nearly a whisper. "Do you remember the boy JoJo?"

"Of course," Sarah replied. "He was beautiful."

"Beautiful?"

"His eyes. So large. You felt they could swallow you."

"Starvation does that. Half the population of Ethiopia has those eyes." Callahan put his cigarette out on the bottom of his boot and tossed the butt out the tent flap. "The boy was my first save here. Ten years old. He was so thin he could hardly stand without help. But even though his system was pretty much completely closed down, he still found the strength to bury the rest of his family. I mean, think about it. How amazing is that?" Callahan shook his head, his expression far away. "Incredible . . . so incredible I can't find words to describe it. I think the point is, we have no idea what courage is. Not the first clue."

"I agree. We'll never know."

Callahan nodded and said, "He used to write me notes. He helped me in the clinic. He was good—you know? He was sweet and he was good and he wanted to be like me. And . . . I liked that . . . it was silly and vain and childish, but it made me feel good about myself. Maybe I could make a difference to one child—one child in the world. . . ." Callahan hesitated and looked away. Sarah could hear his breathing—heavy, strained. "So I took him with me to London—my talisman, my courageous, indomitable Africa . . . Fuck. . . ." There were tears in his eyes, and, seeing them, Sarah fought against tears of her own. "How could I be so bloody stupid? How could I be so totally selfish?"

"Nick . . ."

But he couldn't look at her.

"You were trying to do the right thing."

"I took the boy all that way, then just when he needed me most, just when he was really scared and alone and lost, where was I? I was up to my arse in my own bloody ego. I got separated from him—the one person who could protect him and I wasn't there for him. . . ."

Callahan's voice cracked. His back to Sarah, he lit another cigarette and started digging through an old shoe box in a footlocker underneath his cot. His hands were shaking.

"He wrote me this one note," Callahan said as he searched. "It's here somewhere—about how he was going to be a doctor and how he was going to come back and take my place here."

He finally found it—a small, crumpled piece of paper. He handed it to Sarah. She stared at the cramped, spidery handwriting in a language she could not understand, and yet in her mind's eye she could see his huge, questing eyes and feel his mournful intensity.

"The point is," Callahan continued, "he was my friend. I loved that boy. . . ." He hesitated, unable for a moment to go on.

"I know."

"He had a name. So now I have to remember him. If everyone I lose has a name . . ."

He shook his head, tears streaming down his face; he made no attempt to hide them now. He was unable to speak and Sarah stood beside him gripping the note and aching to touch him, to let him know that feeling what he was feeling was all right. The dam had burst. It was all flooding in now, all the pressure he had built up. So painful, she thought. And yet so necessary.

Minutes passed as they stood there in his tent together, the only sound his weeping. Finally he wiped his hand across his face and looked up.

Sarah smiled—smiled for him—pity and desire gleaming from her eyes.

"I'm sorry," she said. "I wish there was something I could do."

"You're here," he said. "You're listening. That's enough." He managed a faint smile. "I guess this has been coming on for a long time. Sort of incubating—like a tropical fever."

They exchanged a glance that was so poignant with unexpressed feelings that they had to look away. A moment longer and their world could have collapsed into a kiss. I could love this man, Sarah thought in wonder. Maybe I already do.

"So," Callahan said, "if we have to close up shop, what's next for you? Your husband must miss you."

Deftly, he had managed to shift them back into the neutral territory of marriage, responsibility, departure.

"I guess the next stop is home," she answered. She added with a sly grin, "Back to that silly trivial existence you love to ridicule."

"I do, don't I?"

"You do."

"It's my anger," he said. "My sense of outrage. It fuels me. Without it I wonder what I'd be."

"Maybe one day you'll find out."

He nodded. "Right . . ." They stood close, in uneasy silence. Then: "Is it Henry—is that his name? Your husband?"

"Yes."

"He must be terribly proud of you."

"I'm not sure that he is. He was set against my coming here. I think he considered it a crazy, quixotic whim."

"A prudent man," Callahan said. "It takes a streak of insanity to want to be here doing what we're doing."

"You have that streak," she said. "So do I."

He looked deep into her eyes. "I guess you do."

In the silence that followed, Sarah watched as he stared at her mouth, then stole a furtive look at her breasts. She was certain that he was going to pull her toward him in an embrace, that he was about to kiss her. Then what would she do? Would she return the kiss? Did she want this man to kiss her? She was afraid that she did want it—more than anything she wanted it, no matter where it might lead. But then the moment passed.

He said, "Well, it's very late. We'd both better get some sleep."

"Yes."

"Ningpopo—Nincompoop—he's not going to come through, you know."

"I gather that."

"This caravan is going to have to move on. And you need to return to your life in London."

She nodded. "I guess I do."

"Your husband must miss you," he said for the second time.

"Yes," she said.

He reached for her hand, held it for an instant, then shook it.

"Good night," he said.

"Good night."

She stepped toward the tent flap. As she bowed her head to go through, he spoke to her—so softly the words were nearly lost.

"You've been great. We all owe you an enormous debt."

She turned. He was smiling. Nick Callahan had actually complimented her.

She held on to his lovely, warm smile for an instant, then turned, ducked through the tent flap, and was gone.

Dawn came with its usual gravity—hot, heavy air enclosed the camp in its humid embrace. The cloudless sky lightened as one by one, like nightlights being extinguished, the multitude of stars went out. Rising from a dilapidated, makeshift mosque came the mournful wail of the morning call to prayer. As she listened, Sarah shivered. The call to prayer affected her deeply; it spoke of the strength of belief in the face of heartbreak, loss, hunger, and death—and yet curiously it consoled her in a way the rituals of her own religion never had. After all was taken away from you, there still was God. He would not abandon you. You had been tested and now He would take you in his arms at the final moment and transport you to paradise. On this day—her last at the refugee camp—the prayers were particularly poignant, because she had taken into her heart the losses and tragedies of these people and she suspected that she would carry them with her for the rest of her life.

Dressed in her traveling outfit—a gray cotton skirt, white blouse, and sensible black walking shoes—Sarah stepped into the pediatric ward. She crossed to Abraha's cot where he lay sleeping. For a moment she stood over him, smiling to herself. He was still far too thin, but his color had improved, his eyes were clear. In a few short days he had been transformed into an alert little boy, showing curiosity about his growing world. She leaned close to him and kissed his cheek and forehead. She whispered, "Bye-bye, sweet one. I will always love you and you will always be a part of me. Live long. . . ." She spoke those words to him in Tigreyan. Tula, with whom she had developed a bond of respect if not true cordiality, had taught her a few simple phrases in her native language so that she could communicate with the child.

As Sarah approached the van that would take her to the airport, Elliot was loading her luggage into the back. She was surprised—and pleased— to see that Tula would be her driver.

"All ready to go?" Elliot said, looking up with a smile.

"Yes. As ready as I'll ever be."

"Did you say good-bye to your boy?"

Sarah nodded. "With a heavy heart."

Elliot could see how hard she was fighting not to cry. Smiling cheerfully, he said, "Do me a favor when you get back."

"Anything, Elliot."

"Go to a superb restaurant and order roast beef—make sure it's rare—Yorkshire pudding and a fine bottle of claret. As you're eating and drinking, think of me."

She squeezed his hand. "A promise."

He brought out a crumpled business card and handed it to her.

"You should have this," he said. "This is the number of a friend of mine at UNHCR, in London. If you ever need to know where we are, or you think we're so great you want to join up— well, all you have to do is holler."

She read the card and put it in her handbag. "Thank you. I know we'll stay in touch."

"You made a difference," he said. "The boy . . . It's not just all about numbers. It all counts. Every life that's saved—not forgetting to care." He removed the knot of eternity from around his neck. "This is for you. It's your time to wear it."

"Are you sure?"

"I'm sure."

"But I'm not a Buddhist, Elliot."

"In your heart you are."

She fingered it gently. "I'll wear it every day."

"You'd better," he said with a grin. "I'll know if you don't."

He placed it over her head.

"Thank you so much," she said. "This is an honor."

"No, no," he said. "I need to thank you. *Yekenelay*—that means 'thanks.' And you say *genzebka*, which means 'you're welcome.'"

"*Genzebka.*"

"Very good. Very Buddhist. I may have to recruit you."

"Do Buddhists hug?" she said.

"It's been known to happen. Especially among American Buddhists. I hug everything."

They held each other, their cheeks touching, and then Sarah moved around to the front of the van. He could see her eyes searching.

"Nick's up at the well," he said. "You want me to go get him?"

"No, it's okay. Just say . . . good-bye."

"I will."

"And Elliot?"

"Yes?"

"Take care of him."

"That's a tall order," Elliot said with a grin.

"But I know you'll try."

"I'll try my damndest."

"He needs you more than he realizes."

"I know that."

"So . . ." She opened the passenger door. "I'm off now. Bye-bye."

"Good-bye, Sarah."

"We need to move now, baby woman," Tula said impatiently. "You be late for plane."

Callahan, who was working alongside Joss and Ribs, glanced up as the van moved off in a swirl of dust, disappearing into the vastness of the desert. Gradually, as he stood leaning on his shovel, a slow rumble filled the air, growing in intensity. There was a sudden explosion of water erupting from the earth, raining down on everyone. Joss, Ribs, Callahan, and a pack of laughing, shouting children were drenched. In his joy, Joss did a rain dance to the delight of the children.

The van was now no more than a dark dot in the distance. Water pouring from his face, Callahan continued to stare after it.

PART
2

PART

2

As Sarah thought back on it many years later, her life went on hold the day she left the refugee camp and flew back to London. The five years that followed were a blur, punctuated by a few peaks—the birth of her son Jimmy, and her work with the United Nations allocating money for relief to third world countries. But, as she realized later, there were so few other memories, so few memorable moments. It was as though her heart was still with Nick and Elliot and their mission. At first, her reunion with Henry amounted to a second honeymoon, and within weeks she was pregnant. The balance of power in their relationship, however, had shifted since her time in the desert. Increasingly she made decisions about money matters and how they spent their leisure time. She was reluctant to party with Henry's friends and tried to involve him in serious discussions about the state of the world. For the first time she took an interest in politics, and, according to her father-in-law, was becoming a "regular renegade." He would say this to friends with fond condescension. He was very taken with Sarah, secretly considering her a lucky catch for his son, but he found it difficult to respect the mind of any woman—especially a young and beautiful one.

At Sarah's urging, Henry started a consulting business, helping small businesses secure loans from the government. Her secret goal was to wean him from his father. She felt that Henry's reliance on Lawrence Bauford was unhealthy and prevented him from developing a true sense of independence.

The business prospered for a brief period, but Henry's interest soon flagged and he began to lose clients. After a year he was ready to call it quits and return to his father's banking business, but all of Europe had entered an economic downturn, stocks had fallen, and investment banks were laying off workers. There was no longer a place for Henry in the Bauford banking interests. Lawrence Bauford extended his son a low-interest personal loan and urged him to pursue a career teaching business and marketing. He felt that his son was well suited for the academic world, where his passive, reflective nature could prove an asset. Henry's attempts to secure a teaching position, though, were sporadic and halfhearted. The years passed. Henry took a number of retail sales positions—some of them purely on commission—but none of them panned out. With each setback his confidence sank lower. He, Sarah, and the child were reduced to living frugally on Sarah's salary. By 1989, Henry was living under a cloud of chronic depression. Not yet forty, he felt old and considered himself a failure. He helped out around the house, went job hunting when prodded by Sarah, and loved spending time with young Jimmy. More and more the boy was his chief solace in a life of small defeats.

One day in the spring of 1989, Henry rode the bus into London to answer an advertisement for a position with the accounting department at Harrods department store. On his way to the interview he studied his face in the grimy window. He knew that he was still handsome, that he still had the old winning smile, but there was something in his eyes—he could see it even in the dull reflection—something haunted and curiously insubstantial. He tried a smile at his reflection: There was a desperate pleading in it. Like me! Accept me! He had to admit that he looked like a muted version of his former self. The last five years had taken a tremendous toll on his reserves of confidence, leaving him feeling irrelevant. He had had to endure too many rejections and it was hard for him to snap back. He knew he was not the kind of man who responded well to challenges. As his belief in himself waned, more and more he kept his anxieties at bay with extended cocktail hours. Alcohol provided him a measure of buoyancy, brought back some of the old confidence—at least for an hour or two.

The interview went poorly. Within minutes he managed to convey to the Harrods personnel director, both by word and attitude, that he was far too good for the position being offered and that if he deigned to accept it, he would do so only on a temporary basis. His manner was hungry and haughty at the same time; his mind was consumed with the need for a drink. The personnel director, he thought, was loathsome—an ill-bred bully. The kind of person Henry had spent most of his life successfully avoiding. Ten minutes into the interview it was apparent that the two men had taken a strong dislike to each other and Henry was abruptly dismissed.

He arrived home at five o'clock that afternoon after a lengthy stopover at a London cocktail lounge. As he approached the house he considered lying to Sarah. He could say that he'd been offered the job and would be starting in two weeks. That would buy him some time—most importantly a reprieve from Sarah's constant badgering. Then, in two weeks, he could tell her that Harrods had made a decision to reduce their staff and that he was the odd man out. Little lies were becoming easier and easier to tell; at first he had felt some compunction about lying to Sarah, but soon he felt that the lies were a necessary defense against her nagging. Even though Henry was still very much in love with her, he had come to fear her almost as much as he loved her. He was concerned that their lovemaking had suffered recently, and he knew that the fault was his; many times lately he was unable to perform. He blamed "blue feelings" that so often overcame him these days and robbed him of energy. She blamed his drinking.

Henry stared at the house and saw Sarah framed in a lighted window. He pulled his collar closer around his neck against the drizzle. As he continued to stand there, indecisive, he saw his son Jimmy bound past the window clutching a red rubber ball in his hands. Henry saw Sarah's worried frown. "I'm not ready to go in," he muttered to himself. "Not yet. I need time." He moved away slowly into the darkness, away from the lamplight, away from the complaints and questions, no particular destination in mind. Just a walk. Time to think. Time to prepare himself.

The interior of the Bauford house was filled with clutter and half-completed tasks. Most of their good furniture had gone into storage when they moved to a smaller apartment two years ago. Jimmy's plastic toys were strewn around the living room, the beds upstairs were unmade, dirty laundry spilled out of the hamper in the kitchen and the sink and countertop were piled with unwashed dishes. It was not a happy clutter, but instead reeked of depressive disorder.

Jimmy Bauford, aged five, went bounding up the stairs, giving a loud war whoop as he ran. His hair, damp from a bath, was standing up in blond spikes, his pajama bottoms had slipped well down on his buttocks. Flying a Duplo rocket as though his life depended on it, he leaped onto his parents' bed, jumped up and down making growling noises and hurled himself at the pillows, yelling "Yeeeee-*yowww* . . ."

"Jimmy," Sarah called. She appeared in the doorway holding her son's pajama top. She sighed wearily. She had worked all day and now she had to deal with this bundle of superhuman energy. The Bauford's helper, Emily Stallings, was supposed to have left at three, but Henry hadn't arrived home from his interview, which meant that the girl had stayed on an extra two hours until Sarah came home. Which meant extra pay for the girl, and they could ill afford that. Every penny was being pinched these days. Where *was* Henry? It was now seven-thirty. She hoped that his lateness meant good news. Maybe he had landed the job with Harrods and they would have something to celebrate. God knows, they needed something to celebrate.

"Sweetheart, it's way past your bedtime," she said. "Time to go to your bedroom now."

"Want to stay here."

"Well, just for a few minutes."

"Under the covers."

She sighed. "Okay. Under the covers."

Sarah looked as beautiful as the day she had married Henry, but paler, thinner, more fractious. A new line—a line of tension—ran between her eyes, and her hair was awry, unkempt. She was out of the habit of taking the usual care with her appearance.

She stepped forward and reached for Jimmy. He wriggled out of her grasp as she tried to wrestle him into his pajama top.

"I-don't-want-to-go-to-bed-don't-want-to-go-to-bed-don't-want-to-go-to-bed," he squealed in a singsong voice.

She looked into his eyes—Henry's eyes, pale-blue, clear, and beautiful—and felt her heart flood with love. It was impossible to stay angry with this child for more than a moment.

"Jimmy," she said. "Come on, sweetie, please— if you want to stay here, under the covers. I'm going to count to five. One . . . two . . . three . . . four . . ." She knew that she wasn't getting through to him. He was at his most manic at bedtime, and like his father he could appear stone deaf when there was something he didn't want to hear.

"All right," she said with a sigh. "Put your own top on. I'll read you two chapters."

"Three," he said promptly.

"Three then," she agreed.

"And you put my jammies on."

He stuck his arms up, grinning. Sarah grinned back, defeated, adoring, wracked by conflicting emotions—love for her son and fear for the future of her family.

"You are nothing but a minxish-minx, young man." She ran a hand through his thick hair.

"Mishish mish," he repeated. "You, too, Mom. You are very mishish."

Henry stepped quietly through the door into the bedroom, pulling off his wet coat, smoothing down his wet hair.

"You should leave that downstairs," Sarah said in greeting. "It's dripping."

"Sorry."

"You're late," she said.

"Hello there," he said. "Certainly appreciate the greeting. Your coat is dripping and you're late."

She stiffened as he kissed her cheek.

Jimmy jumped up and down on the bed excitedly. "Daddy—Mummy says I can have *three* chapters tonight. Did you know I'm a mishish?"

"A minx, sweetie."

"Three chapters?" Henry said to his son. "Excellent. Every boy should be read three chapters before sleep. Three is the perfect number."

He gave Sarah a smile, which she didn't return.

"Would you mind reading to him? I need to do some work."

"Be glad to. Jim? Into your room and under the covers. Daddy will be there in two seconds. Quick-sticks. Off you go now."

The child hurtled out of the room with a resounding war whoop.

"Good to see someone happy," Henry said as he watched him go.

"Yes, isn't it."

He turned his gaze on her for the first time, but failing to catch her eye he quickly glanced away. "What's he reading?"

"It's on the bedside table."

"About the job . . ." He waited.

"Well? Did you get it?"

"No," he said, deciding just then not to lie. What was the use? He would be raising her spirits only to dash them later. "They wanted a woman," he added, opting for a littler lie.

"The ad didn't say that."

"The adverts don't tell you everything."

She shrugged and said resignedly, "Too bad."

"Listen," he said, "about tomorrow . . ."

Sarah, sensing the question, answered quickly. "I'm in the office all day."

"It's just—well, I need to do more job hunting. Something's bound to break soon."

"I thought you were going to make calls from home."

"Yes. But I really ought to go in. Half the city's looking for work. I can't compete unless I'm there."

"Can't your father help you? I don't understand your reluctance to go to him."

Henry shook his head fiercely. "The bank is out. The work I used to do—and John Grooms, he used to be my assistant—it's all being handled by one woman now." He added with an edge of bitterness, "Consolidation is the new hot button word. Get one person to do the work of two. Let the other fellow starve."

"But I'm sure he would help you."

"If you mean another loan, you can forget it. He's already loaned me more than he can afford. Dad was hit pretty hard by the recession."

"I know that. Though I'm sure he's still better off than most."

"It's all relative, Sarah. He's not a pauper exactly. But he used to be well-to-do." Henry hesitated, then said, "So . . . I think I should go in."

Sarah's lower lip pushed out, a sure sign that she was ready to do battle.

"Henry, I arranged meetings, especially because you promised you'd do the school run. I can't change things at your whim."

"I would hardly call a job search a whim."

"Listen," she said wearily, "I'm not going to stand here arguing. My schedule is set for tomorrow. It's too late to change it."

"Well, can't we ask somebody to come in? What about Emily? I'm sure she can move things around."

"She has a second job."

"There must be people at school who could take him and pick him up."

"Fine," she said, an edge in her tone. "You call them. I'm fed up asking favors of people I hardly know."

They faced each other in tense silence. Shaking her head, Sarah bent down and picked up his dirty socks.

"Here—give me those. I'll take them downstairs."

"Never mind. I'll collect all the dirty clothes scattered around and start a wash."

"I can do the wash," he said.

"But you didn't," she snapped. "You had plenty of time in the morning before your interview. Nothing got done. The dishes stacked in the sink, the beds unmade. God knows what you do while Jimmy's in school and I'm at work. Watch the telly, read novels, sleep?"

Henry reached for the dirty socks again. "I'm only trying to help, Sarah."

"No you're not. You're bargaining with me."

Henry stared at her, feeling the now familiar depression. It darkened his mind and left him weak. When a man runs out of options . . . When a man has nothing to look forward to . . . When a man's own wife . . . But he was incapable of completing those thoughts. He wished he had kept walking in the rain and had not come home.

"And what if I was?" he said finally, his voice barely above a whisper. "Is that such a terrible crime? There are worse things, you know. I could argue and shout and throw my weight around. What good would that do? What would we solve?" He tightened his lips to keep them from trembling. "I hate not having a job. You don't know how much I hate it. It makes me feel small and stupid—less than a man. I hate that feeling. There's nothing in this world I want more than to be able to support you and Jimmy. A man needs to be a successful breadwinner—it satisfies deep cravings. Otherwise what is he? The thing is, we mustn't make each other feel worse than we already do."

Henry reached for her hand; hers felt lifeless, unresponsive.

"Sarah?"

She continued to shake her head. "Look at this room. It's a mess."

"We'll sort it out," he said, and knew when he said the words that he wasn't talking about the room.

"No, Henry. *You* will. You're here and I'm working. This is your responsibility now. I'm sick of writing out lists—'Do this, do that.' You're a big boy. You should be able to do things on your own without being told."

"Oh, I didn't tell you," he said, trying for an upbeat tone. "Apparently there's some East European chap who's big in futures. I'm going to arrange a meeting with him." He squeezed her hand. "We'll sort it out, sweetheart. I know we will."

"Jimmy's waiting for you to read to him," she said, withdrawing her hand.

Henry looked at her for a moment and then walked out of the room.

Sarah's office at UNHCR was in a nondescript building, with one sluggish and temperamental elevator. The view from her single large window, however, was spectacular. She could look down across the Thames and see the dome of St. Paul's in the distance. Early the next morning, damp and drizzly, she stood at the window, her phone tucked in her shoulder, scribbling on an envelope as she talked.

"Sure," she said. "I understand what you're saying, but you know you're exaggerating. We send—"

"I am *not* exaggerating," the voice insisted, whiny and educated. "You give us a pittance. What do we have to do to unlock your loaded vaults?"

Sarah sighed as she strode to her desk where a

mountain of paperwork awaited her. "Michael, this is bullshit—excuse me—and you know it. The UNHCR sends more aid to Honduras than the rest of the UN put together. Most people don't even know where Honduras is, for Christ's sake."

"North of Panama," he said dryly, "on the Caribbean Sea."

"Very funny, Michael."

"I trust you're not going to leave us high and dry," he said. "The country is in big trouble, the economy's stalled—at a total standstill. The infant death rate is rising daily."

"I know all that," she said. "It's the story of more third world nations than I can count."

The small television set on Sarah's desk, mounted precariously on a bundle of government reports, showed images of East and West Berliners tearing down the wall. Sarah's sister Charlotte was talking directly to the camera, the joyous crowds serving as a backdrop behind her. In the past five years Charlotte's star had risen fast, and six months earlier CNS had hired her as one of their top foreign reporters.

The volume was turned down and Sarah strained to hear her sister's words.

"Michael," she said into the phone, "I'll see what I can do. Call me in two weeks."

"I hope you're not giving us the runaround."

"I'll do my best," she said. "That's a promise.

But just keep in mind, the money stream isn't endless."

"Nothing is, but please try," he said, and hung up.

Sarah sat at her desk studying Charlotte's performance closely. She had let her hair grow long, which accentuated her natural curls. She looks really fabulous, Sarah thought, feeling a surge of pride. Charlotte had become the darling of CNS watchers everywhere—the intrepid, articulate beauty who reported back from the front lines, wearing a flak jacket, risking her life for the story. Always ravishing. An American publisher had recently offered her a seven-figure advance for a memoir. She was mulling it over.

" . . . What is perhaps most remarkable," she was saying, "is that some of these people are seeing their relatives for the first time in nearly thirty years. The sense you get of hope here, of a fresh beginning, is truly amazing. Behind me, as I speak, East and West Berliners alike are tearing down the greatest symbol of Communist repression for nearly three decades. The Berlin wall is finally coming down." She paused for a dramatic moment before continuing. "November ninth, nineteen eighty-nine—a day that marks the opening up of a remarkable new chapter in world history.

"This is Charlotte Jordan, for CNS in Berlin."

CNS moved on to a breaking story from Israel,

and Sarah clicked off the TV. She stared at the blank screen. "Way to go, Charlie," she said out loud, grinning. "You're kicking ass, big sis'. I always knew you would."

Sarah began to attack the mess of papers strewn across her desk when the telephone rang.

"UNHCR," she said. "Sarah Bauford."

"How impressive. You answer your own phone."

The voice had a familiar ring, but Sarah couldn't place it. "Who is this please?"

"Elliot. Elliot Hauser."

"Elliot," Sarah cried, her face lighting up. "How are you? *Where* are you? What a pleasant surprise."

"Actually I'm calling from a phone booth here in London."

"Wonderful. I'm dying to see you."

"I'm dying to see you too, Sarah. Five years . . ."

"I know. It doesn't seem possible, does it?"

"No. Time just speeds faster and faster."

"Your voice is fading in and out."

"It's a bad connection. Nothing works in this city, does it?"

Sarah laughed. "The sunset of an empire. When can I see you?"

"That depends on you. Can you get away?"

"Sure. Just tell me where you are and I'll be there."

"I'm in the Holland Park tube station. Can we meet by the entrance to the park in a couple of hours?"

"Fine. Hey—it's great to hear your voice."

"Yours, too."

She hung up, her face ablaze with anticipation. A rush of happiness—a rush that she hadn't felt for longer than she cared to think about—flooded her. She had wanted to ask about Nick Callahan but had forced herself not to. He was constantly in her thoughts, and she had had to train herself not to mention his name or refer to him when she related stories about her time in Ethiopia. When she had first returned from Ethiopia she had brought up his name constantly until she realized that she was causing Henry great pain. From then on, Nick Callahan had remained buried but never for a moment forgotten.

The phone rang again almost immediately. Grabbing her coat and briefcase, Sarah yelled through the door, "Chloe, can you get that? Something's come up and I've got to run. See you in the morning."

She took a cab rather than a bus to her house, blowing her budget for the week. She had written an account of her stay in the refugee camp, which she thought would interest Elliot. She had spent hours on it—usually late at night when Henry was sleeping—and rewritten it many times, struggling to polish it to a high level. She had never shown it to anyone—not even Charlotte. It was her secret.

When she arrived at the house, she dumped

her briefcase and paused. A woman's coat was draped over the banister. She looked around, frowning.

"Henry?"

"Is that you, Sarah?" She could hear a faint note of alarm in his voice. "I'm—here in the living room."

He was sitting stiffly, too upright, in a soft armchair. His hands were clasped tightly together. Opposite him, clearly embarrassed, sat Beatrice, the sweet-faced, tangle-haired charity worker from the ball five years earlier. At the time she had been Lawrence Bauford's assistant. Henry had not mentioned her name in years. They both wore strained smiles.

Sarah studied them, making an effort to remain calm. "Henry?" she said again.

He rose, clearing his throat and grinning too brightly.

"Hello, love. Bea just popped round to say hello. She was in the neighborhood. You do remember Bea, don't you? She used to work for Dad."

"Of course. I remember."

Beatrice also rose and extended a hand. "Hello, Sarah."

"Hi," Sarah said, giving the woman's hand a brief shake. She stared intently into her eyes until she looked away, clearly rattled.

"I thought you were job hunting, Henry."

"Cancelled."

"What about Emily?"

"I sent her home."

"Oh."

He continued to clear his throat nervously. "What brings you home so early?"

"I have an appointment," she said. "I'll be out for a few hours." She checked her watch. "You need to pick up Jimmy in half an hour."

"I know."

"Well," she said, "I'll be off. I just came by to pick up some papers." She caught Henry in her gaze and held him pinned. "I'll leave you two alone. . . ."

Sarah sat in Holland Park, staring out into the damp day and seeing nothing. She lit a cigarette and inhaled deeply. What she needed more than anything right now was a stiff drink. Henry was fucking this Beatrice woman. Guilt was written all over them. And Sarah was trying to understand what she felt about that. He had betrayed her—right in their own home, probably in their bed—but then, in her thoughts at least, she had betrayed Henry. Always with the same man. Always with Nick Callahan. How much difference was there between the thought and the deed? She realized that Henry's morale was at a low ebb and that she was doing little to bolster his ego. As an unemployed male in his prime earning years his manhood was being threatened, and instead of showing some understanding, she was bitchy and impatient with him. The fault clearly was not all his, and yet she seethed with anger.

"Sarah . . ."

Elliot Hauser was standing over her, smiling. He looked tan and fit and thinner than she remembered. She rose and held him in a long, heartfelt hug.

"Hello," he said.

"Hello, Elliot. You look exactly the same."

"So do you," he said. But he was too honest a man to lie successfully. She looked tired and somewhat sad. She had definitely aged, although she was still remarkably beautiful.

"I look a wreck," she said with a grin. "But thank you for your kind words."

"Did you get my last letter?" he said quickly, eager to change the subject.

"You were in Pakistan."

"Pakistan?" He looked at her with surprise. "But that was months ago. I haven't written you since then?"

"You're too busy saving lives." She gave him another hug.

He ducked his head in mock modesty. "Of course. The knight on the white charger. Well, we're not in Pakistan anymore. We've moved on to Cambodia, near the Thai border. Doing our bit there . . ." He broke off, looking at her with concern. Her smile was tremulous and dissolving; he could tell that she was on the verge of tears.

"You okay?"

"Fine."

He nodded, probing her with his soft and gentle eyes.

"And Jimmy?"

"Gorgeous."

"Bien sûr."

Sarah looked away, too confused to continue this conversation; she couldn't confide in Elliot because the hurt was too fresh. Until she understood it better she had to deal with it on her own. She moved them along, saying, "You're in London. You call me out of the blue."

"Yes."

She managed a smile. "Would that be because I'm with the United Nations, or because I'd never forgive you if you didn't?"

"Both, to be honest."

"Okay. Tell me what's going on."

"What do you know about Cambodia?"

"Well, they're in the midst of a Civil War—that much I know. Communist coalition forces headed by the Khmer Rouge are running the government and fighting the Communist Vietnamese. I believe the British call it 'political irony.'"

"Nick calls it 'a cluster fuck'," Elliot said. "But you know our Nick. Never one to mince words."

Finally his name was mentioned. Sarah had

used all her self-control not to bring him up first.

"How is he?" she said, trying to keep her tone casual.

When Elliot was slow to respond, she added, "Is he well?"

"He's"—Elliot shrugged—"he's Nick. What can I say?"

Watching him intently, Sarah said, "Was it his idea for you to come and see me?"

"No, no," Elliot replied with an embarrassed laugh. "It was both of us. I mean—well, I wanted to see you anyway. And as you know, I always do the money. Nick can't pitch to save his life. Well, you know that about him. His idea of a pitch is to insult you, yell a little, and then expect you to deliver."

She nodded. "The leopard doesn't change his spots."

"Not that leopard anyway." Elliot hurried on awkwardly. "So . . . I'm sorry—where was I?"

"Cambodia."

"Right. Well, according to Washington the place doesn't officially exist. Currently there's something like half a million people living under Khmer Rouge domination. The death rate averages fifteen to twenty a day in every village. Dysentery, measles, pneumonia . . . No vaccines, of course."

"None at all?"

"None." His smile was weary. "It does sound familiar, doesn't it?"

"Yes."

"Plus, the land mines—lots of land mines. So we have amputees without prosthetics. It's not a happy place, Sarah."

She nodded, her lips compressed in a thin line, all business now.

"What do you need, Elliot?"

He chuckled softly. "I guess you knew I was making a pitch, didn't you?"

"Of course. I know you love me dearly, but more than my charm brought you here. Tell me what you need."

"Well, we recently secured a shipment—vaccines, medicines, food, the usual stuff—but there's a lot of corruption out there. On a par with Ethiopia, if you can believe it. If we could . . ." He broke off.

"Just say it, Elliot."

"Slap a UN stamp on it," he said.

"A UN stamp?"

"The point is, the UN name still means something, even in that hellhole. It would be like a bit of extra protection. Of course we'd take full responsibility. You would do the paperwork. . . ."

Elliot petered out, waiting for a response. Sarah continued to stare at him, expressionless. Thoughts were whirling through her mind. Land mines . . . Children without limbs . . . A country, a people, unrecognized by the most powerful nation on earth. And Nick . . . And Henry . . . What he had done to her. What she now felt compelled to do. Finally, when she spoke, her words were curt and professional.

"We do have shipments going in," she said. "We can attach yours to the list."

Elliot sighed, gripped her hand. "That would be a great help. I can't begin to tell you."

"I'm going to come with the shipment," she said quietly. "I'd like to see this through."

Elliot stared at her, appalled. "Oh, you don't have to do that. Really, Sarah . . ."

"I've done it before. I'm an old hand by now."

"But Cambodia's a sinkhole, the absolute pits. I can't tell you how bad it is—and you have a family—"

"I'll see it through," she said, looking him straight in the eye. "I've made up my mind."

"I can see that."

They sat on the bench, in the soft cool drizzle of a late afternoon, holding hands.

11

S arah arrived in Phnom Penh three weeks later. Unlike her departure five years earlier, Henry put up no resistance. In fact she felt that he was secretly relieved. She had not brought up his relationship with Beatrice, hoping that he would come forward, bring it out in the open, but he had said nothing. The woman stood between them now—an invisible and yet very real physical presence capable of destroying whatever was left of their love and trust. Since the day Sarah had discovered the former charity worker in her home, she and Henry had not touched each other in bed or exchanged so much as a kiss. They were like a pair of overly polite acquaintances. They could not go on this way. Sarah knew that when she returned they would have to sit down, talk seriously, and resolve their relationship one way or the other. The only bright spot on their dark domestic horizon was that Lawrence Bauford had found Henry employment in a competitor's bank. He would start work immediately, and with the extra income they could afford to hire Emily full-time to stay with Jimmy. At least Emily is nothing to look at, Sarah thought grimly. Henry should be able to keep his hands off her.

Phnom Penh, Cambodia, in 1989 was torn apart by civil strife. Food was scarce and riots were a daily occurrence. No one was safe and gunfire was as common as traffic noise. Sarah stood amid the chaos on a decrepit dock struggling to check off her partially unloaded cargo, while half a dozen officials argued with a crowd of dockers in the shadow of a rusted cargo ship. At Sarah's side stood a wild-eyed young interpreter, Tao, limping around excitedly on a prosthetic leg. A Cambodian official had elbowed his way between Sarah and her cargo, talking furiously, frowning, shaking his head. His black eyes looked as though they would burst out of his head. The official screamed at Sarah in broken English, and Tao screamed back at him in Cambodian. "The money don't go in your pocket," Tao said, reverting to English. "Go fuck off, dirty bastard!"

Sarah, dizzy with exhaustion (she hadn't slept in twenty-four hours), stared from one man to the other. She had never heard such an intensity of screaming and had an urge to clap her hands over her ears like a small child. A wave of nausea passed through her. She was jittery from too much strong coffee and too much noise.

"Tao, what's going on?" she said. "Where's Nick? Elliot told me he would be here. What does this man want?"

"Money, Missy Sarah. Money, shit! They see you, this white English woman. You give them more. They want more. That is what you do. They fuck the dockers."

"I'm American," she said.

"American, English. It is always more—more money in the wrong pockets. Ha!" He hopped up and down in agitation. "Wait, wait, wait . . ." He turned to the dockers and yelled in Cambodian, "That's what I tell her. More money—more money in *your* hands. Not that prick bastard. *More for you.* She don't understand. I make her understand."

There was more shouting, counter screams, and fist waving from the angry official, who in awe of Tao's wrath had backed off a few steps. Sarah felt a throbbing in her temples; she was worried that she might faint.

"Just as long as they don't confiscate our stuff," she said to Tao. "Maybe you shouldn't be screaming at them. Just say no more money."

Tao spun around on her, the whites of his black eyes red with rage. "What you say?"

"Tell them I'm not paying any more. But if you can do it without antagonizing them—"

"They want more money," he interrupted.

"I understand, Tao. Tell them they've already had their ten percent. It's written in the contract."

"No, no," Tao snapped. "Contract, shit! This Cambodia, Missy. Contract is shit. They say you pay." He spun around again and shouted at the dockers, "I'm telling her, you fuck faces. But she not hearing me."

"What did you say?"

"I'm saying they insist on more money."

"No. Absolutely not."

"Missy Sarah—"

"They've got their money."

"They need more," he shouted. "You pay! You no say no! This is stinking poor country."

"Christ," Sarah said through gritted teeth, staring at the coastal road. "Where the hell is Nick?" Turning back to Tao she said, "You tell them now. They've been paid what the contract called for. Either they take the rest of the shipment off the boat or I'll—"

"Or you will what? *What? What you do?* This not Chelsea football. This Cambodia. They say you pay, you pay!"

"The hell I will," Sarah said and stormed away. But the agitated Cambodian limped after her, gesticulating wildly.

"You pay," he shouted. "You pay! You pay! You pay!"

Nearly three hours later, two trucks, belching smoke, crawled up the crazily packed avenue in Phnom Penh. Not on the busiest day in London or New York City had Sarah ever seen such congestion. The traffic consisted of trucks, cars, buses, motorbikes, bicycles, and pedestrians—all following some mad logic of their own. A blue haze of auto emissions blanketed the street. The air was toxic, and Sarah rolled up the window all the way.

Tao drove in the Cambodian style, recklessly and screaming at everyone and everything in his way. Sarah sat beside him, weary and humiliated. She had paid off the dockers and hated herself for giving in.

Tao was mumbling under his breath, still furious with her. "Why you not pay when I say, Missy Sarah? Huh? I tell you how is done here. *I* say how it is, and you not listen to Tao. You listen next time, huh? No more fuck up with Tao."

"Why wasn't Nick there to meet me?" she said after a brooding silence. "I was told he would come."

"Doctor Nick busy man. He meet us soon. You go upriver by boat now, long way."

Sarah stared out the window, too drained to fight. She closed her eyes, and even with the jostling and racket of the truck she was asleep in seconds.

That same afternoon Callahan and Jan Steiger stood at the counter of a busy side street bar in Phnom Penh sipping beers. It was typical of bars in that city: neon-lit, crammed with Vietnamese soldiers, bar girls, some mercenaries, and a ragged band playing American golden oldies. The noise was deafening.

"I don't have much time," Callahan said. "I'm already late to meet a shipment."

"We don't need much time," Steiger said. "You must know why I asked to meet you here."

"Enlighten me."

Steiger smiled. He had gained a great deal of weight in the past five years and folds of fat connected his face and throat, giving him the look of a man without a chin.

"You know, I was here in 'sixty-five. The place was paradise. Anything you wanted you could buy—and buy at a bargain. Now it's fucking paradise lost. Did you know the river here runs backward in the monsoon? Can you believe that?"

A chubby girl, no more than seventeen, sidled up to Steiger and put her arm through his. Callahan's eyes did not waver from Steiger's face. His voice low and serious, he said, "Let's cut to the chase here. I just blew all my credibility with the

UN getting this load through. It's two weeks late. What the hell's going on?"

"You know perfectly well what's going on. The crates were delayed so I could get them properly fitted." He sipped his beer and regarded Callahan mockingly. 'What's going on?' Come on, my friend, stop with the whining. We're in the final innings, pal. Moscow's closing the books on the Viets, the Chinese are closing theirs on the Khmer Rouge. This country's a rat fuck, up for grabs. . . ."

"'A rat fuck,'" the chubby girl said, giggling. Steiger massaged her stomach and made kissing motions with his fat lips. "You can listen," he said softly, "but shut up, okay?"

"Do you have any idea how fast this measles epidemic spreads in two weeks?" Callahan said.

Steiger gave an elaborate shrug. "I've got other stains on my laundry, great white doctor. You're not my only child." He slid along the countertop a crumpled brown envelope. Without glancing at it, Callahan stuffed it in his pocket.

"Twenty-five thousand," Steiger said. "Tell that sorry little excuse for a colonel that's twenty-five more than he deserves."

Callahan fingered his pocket uneasily. "I'm telling you, Steiger, if anything goes wrong I won't have Sarah Bauford involved."

"Bringing the girl was a dumb idea. I can't understand why you allowed it."

Callahan suddenly snapped. "Bullocks, then! I don't want the fucking money." He removed the envelope from his pocket and dropped it in front of Steiger. "I'm not going to kill people for you," he went on. "No way. That's not in my plan."

Steiger impatiently pushed the girl away—she was nuzzling up to his shoulder making purring sounds—the better to concentrate on Callahan.

"Nobody's asking you to kill anybody," he said. "You've got the medicine. So just deliver the fucking crates. Now how complicated can that be?"

Callahan slammed his beer bottle down on the counter. "Fuck you, Steiger. I have a conscience."

"Conscience?" Steiger said, laughing. "The man has a conscience? That's very interesting, Nick my boy. What about Ethiopia?"

"Another beer," Callahan said to the bartender.

"What about Ethiopia? Where was your conscience then? On vacation?"

"I introduced you to a few rebels and gave you some information. That was it. End of story."

"So what's the matter?" Steiger said. "You scared now all of a sudden? You getting religion? I mean Christ, man, you're just shipping some toys we bought off the Vietnamese. No numbers, no bill of sale. We're clean."

"That's not the point. I happen to know what's in those fucking crates of yours, and I don't like it. I'm out."

Steiger's jaw tightened and his beady eyes grew

smaller. "You're out? I hope I'm not hearing you right."

"You are."

"Well, if you're out, my friend, then you'd better know this. I will bury you ten feet deep, you and your fucking colleagues. I will expose you for what you are, and I'll make it look ten times worse than it is. You'll be run out of this fucking profession in disgrace."

With the tips of his fingers he slid the envelope in front of Callahan.

"Let's get something straight. I'm the guy who makes you possible. Without me, you don't exist and a whole lot of people die. You owe me, Nicky boy. You owe me big time. So what you're going to do is, you're going to take the money. You will do this and you will do it *right.*"

Callahan stared straight ahead at his image in the smudgy bar mirror. He did not answer.

"You want to know what it means to be a humanitarian?" Steiger said. "It means making compromises. It means playing the game, getting your hands dirty. Humanitarians are not angels, and you, of all people, should know that. So don't sit there and give me some shit about shades of moral right and wrong. It bores me."

Callahan said nothing.

"Your problem is, you ask too many questions. You have too many scruples. This isn't the Boy

Scouts, my friend." He raised his beer bottle. "Welcome to the real world."

Tao drove slowly along a badly rutted road bordered with sugar palms. Sarah and Tao had barely spoken during the trip. She kept drifting in and out of sleep. As they bumped along, she noticed him adjust his prosthetic leg. Tao saw her glance and grinned.

"What happened to you?" she asked.

"I was sick, Missy Sarah," he replied. "I had bad lung. TB. At this time, no doctors where I live. Khmer Rouge kill all doctors. KR kill my grandfather, some cousins. So . . . I walk to border for medicine. But I must cross minefield." Tao shook his head vigorously as though in agreement with himself, keeping his eyes on the road to avoid the larger potholes. "You never forget the sound. First thing you hear is click. The click is your foot priming the land mine. Soon as you hear it, it's over. But your mind go crazy, you know? You thinking, Maybe if I jump—maybe if I reach out for a rock to match my weight. But is nothing you can do. Once you hear the click—big bye-bye." He grinned, glancing quickly at her. "I was lucky. Just lost my leg."

"That is a terrible story," she said.

"Not so terrible. I am alive."

As Tao continued driving, now wrapped in silence, Sarah fell into a deep sleep, and was still sleeping as the first pink of dawn lit the sky. Tao pulled up to a riverside dock. He eased himself out of the truck, stretched, and limped over to Callahan who was waiting on the bank. They shook hands.

"Any problems?" Callahan said.

"Missy Sarah argue with the dockers about pay-off. I set her straight. She is strong-minded woman." He grinned.

Callahan nodded. "The trucks upriver—are they set?"

"They be there to meet you, boss."

Callahan glanced at the truck. "Did she ask a lot of questions?"

"No. She slept most of the way. She ask me about my leg."

Callahan lit a cigarette. "I guess I should say hello to her."

"I guess you should, boss," Tao said with a grin.

"What's so funny, Tao? Let me in on the joke."

"I smile because I'm happy," Tao replied. "Why not?"

Callahan took a deep drag on his cigarette, then put it out under his boot. He walked to the truck and stared at Sarah Bauford through the passenger window. Five years . . . Five long years . . . And here she is. Five years and more etched on her face, but she was as beautiful as ever to Callahan. Looking down at her, his heart gave a lurch.

As he continued to stare she slowly came awake. A slow smile spread across her face as she squinted at him, silhouetted against the dawn light. She yawned, covering her mouth with a hand. He opened the door and she stepped out. For a moment neither of them knew what to do or say. Finally Callahan extended an arm and they shook hands.

He grinned. "You're not wearing your perfume."

"You look good, Nick. You've lost weight."

"No four-star restaurants in the vicinity." As he continued to look at her, he shook his head. "Five years. I can't believe it."

"Neither can I." She stifled another yawn and looked around, trying to get her bearings. There was a sleepy grandeur to the Mekong, the quiet banks, the steady putt-putt of boats pushing upriver.

"Where were you?" she said. "Elliot said you would meet me."

"Sorry. I had some business to take care of."

They stared at each other, drinking in features that they had seen so often in their dreams. It was difficult for them to believe they were actually together again after so many years, having lived a secret life in each other's thoughts and desires.

"Are you going to tell me where we're headed?" Sarah said, breaking away from his gaze.

"A camp not far from Pailin. By the border."

"And boat's the best way to travel?"

Callahan pretended to be hurt. "Come on, ma'am, you don't like my boat?"

Sarah grinned. "Well, let's just say it's different."

"It's safer to travel by boat," he explained. "You avoid roadblocks, the Khmer Rouge, plus other assorted crazies. Cambodia is crawling with them. You know—heart-of-darkness land."

"Is it really that bad?"

"It's worse," he said. "Actually it's a nightmare."

"I got that impression from Elliot. And yet he seemed pretty upbeat."

Callahan smiled, his heart strangely light. He was happy to be near her again.

"Well, Elliot is Elliot. All he does is give you the Buddhist version. Yes, there's the killing and the corruption, but look at those beautiful temples and the gentlefolk tending the land and cultivating their spiritual side. All complete bullocks. This place is your complete bad dream, in bloody Technicolor. The Khmer Rouge—rouge being very much the appropriate color—use Pailin as a hideout. They keep women there as baby-making factories and the kids as minesweepers."

"Jesus, Nick."

"Yeah—real nice folks. Oh, and in case we actually help anybody, they steal everything we can't hide."

"Why do they even let you stay?"

"Simple. They need doctors."

They let the silence settle over them, happy to be together again. When they heard a boat plying the river, Nick said, "Maybe I should be singing 'Old Man River.'" He tried a few notes in his deep baritone voice, decidedly off-key.

"Then again, maybe you shouldn't," Sarah said, wincing comically. "Nick . . ." She took his hand again. "It's really, really good to see you."

"You, too," he said. "This time around I'll try to be on my best behavior."

"Oh, I doubt that." She squeezed his hand. "We'll see."

12

An hour later, Callahan and Tao were fueling the boat and preparing to load it from the trucks when they discovered that the hull was badly damaged and taking water. Their plans underwent a quick change: They would have to risk traveling on land. There was no other choice. By noon, the convoy of three trucks, fully loaded, was prepared to set out for the refugee camp, Tao driving the lead truck with Callahan sitting beside him. Sarah was riding in the truck behind. They drove for nearly an hour when they pulled up to a roadblock in a cloud of red dust. Callahan climbed down, followed by Tao.

Vietnamese soldiers were sprawled around on the ground in the hot sun. Colonel Gau, a gaunt, sour man, hatless with thinning hair, waited for Callahan to approach. His own concept of protocol prevented him from moving even a step forward in greeting. Gau gripped a car antenna and held it stiffly at his side. His darting eyes flicked from Callahan to Tao.

Colonel Gau snapped out an order in Vietnamese to his soldiers. They moved to check out the contents of the trucks as Callahan ambled over to Gau, bestowing on the small grim man his brightest and most charming smile. He offered the colonel a six-pack of beer and a carton of Camel cigarettes.

"Colonel Gau," he said, "good to see you again."

Not a word from Gau, not even a change of expression. He stared at the gifts which Callahan held out to him and slowly shook his head no. He waved them away with his car antenna.

Sarah emerged from the second truck, nervous and bewildered. She watched as Callahan offered the Colonel Steiger's crumpled brown envelope. This gift Gau accepted with a stiff jerk of his head.

"No trucks," Gau said in painfully enunciated English. "They get in wrong hands."

"Colonel—did I ever bullshit you? I give you my word—these supplies go only to women and children. I stay as far away as I can from the Khmer Rouge."

The Colonel said curtly, "I tell you, no more

trucks. I cannot allow that." His eyes remained fixed on Callahan. "You go back," he said. "You go back now."

Callahan stared at him, puzzled. "What the hell is your problem, Gau? I made my delivery. What are you doing?"

The Colonel waved him away dismissively and walked stiffly, ramrod straight, over to the trucks, joining the soldiers who were pulling out crates of supplies and chopping into them.

Callahan, suddenly panicked, yelled out, "Hey, take it easy. That's medicine, for Christ's sake. It's fragile."

Sarah approached the truck. "What's going on, Nick? I don't understand."

He waved her back. "Stay out of it."

Tao was speaking to the Colonel in Vietnamese, gesticulating wildly, fawning and bowing. Ignoring Tao, the Colonel pointed to one of the larger crates, which had been thrown onto the ground. A soldier crossed over with an ax. Gau looked at Callahan, his expression suspicious and grim. "Let's see what you have here, Doctor Callahan."

Callahan shrugged. "Go ahead."

"Nick—don't let them do this," Sarah called out. "They have no right."

"There's no way to stop them," he said.

The soldier swung at the crate, splintering the wood. He reached inside and pulled out a cello-phane-wrapped load of prosthetics.

"Why are they doing this?" Sarah said to Callahan. He did not reply or shift his eyes from the soldier with the ax. He was bent over the crate removing IV sacs, powdered milk, antimalarials, BP-5 food biscuits, and various bottles of pills. He stopped and looked at the Colonel.

"Proceed," he said.

"You can see what's there," Callahan said.

The Colonel said, "I want to see more." He instructed the soldier to remove the rest.

The soldier tore away more straw and removed a laptop computer. Everyone stared at it. Gau barked an order and the soldier handed him the computer. He held it at arm's length and squinted at it suspiciously. He then rested it on the hood of the lead truck and poked at it with a finger, his curiosity aroused. He turned to Callahan and said, "What is this machine?"

"A computer," Callahan answered. "Every NGO's got one. That's the way we do business." Seeing a soldier heaving IV sacs on the ground, Callahan said, "Jesus, Gao, tell them to take it easy. They can't throw those away. People's lives depend on them, for fuck's sake."

The soldier with the ax approached another crate.

"Come on, Colonel," Callahan pleaded. "You've examined one crate. Isn't that enough? You don't have to open them all."

The ax came down, splitting open another

large crate. The soldier, grunting with exertion, pulled out a heavy bore-hole drilling unit. He dropped it on the ground.

The Colonel pointed at it as he looked at Callahan.

"It's for finding water," Callahan explained, making an effort to hide his growing impatience.

"This is a farce," Sarah muttered under her breath. She stepped forward and said, "Colonel Gau? I'm with UNHCR—the United Nations. You understand that this cargo is protected by international law, and any tampering—"

Callahan spun toward her and said, "Stay out of this, Sarah. Let me handle it, okay?" His voice was thick with tension.

She shook him off angrily and said to Gau, "If this shipment is harmed, your name will surface in a follow-up investigation. I don't think you want that."

She froze as the soldier who was inspecting the crate began removing Russian-made night goggles, night satellite compasses, and more intricate technical equipment which Sarah did not recognize. Stunned, she gave Callahan a questioning glance, but he looked away.

Colonel Gau leaned over the crate, inspecting various items. He reached deeper into the crate and pulled out a Kalishnikov rifle. He held it up as he stared at Callahan. "Explain, please," he said.

Callahan spread his arms in apparent disbelief.

"Look, I have no idea how this stuff got here. Somebody must have mixed up the shipments. Or tampered with the crates. I don't know."

Colonel Gau, still bent over the crate, removed a paper manual. He began to leaf through it. He muttered under his breath as he read. When he finally looked up, his black eyes burned with hatred.

"You can try to explain this, Doctor Callahan. This act of treason." The manual was entitled *Order of Battle* and detailed all aspects of the Vietnamese evacuation—maps, locations, lists of weapons. He tapped the manual. "It is all here." He stood, icy white, staring, a slight tremor in his hands. "Well? What can you say? Can you give me any reason for this?"

Callahan shook his head slowly. "I can't, Colonel. I had nothing to do with this."

"It is your shipment. You take responsibility."

"Look, Gau, what's the problem? Just keep what you want to keep and let me go with the food and drugs. People are dying—your people. My job is to save lives here, and nothing else matters."

"Nothing else matters?" the Colonel screamed. He jumped forward with surprising agility and whipped the car antenna viciously across Callahan's face.

Howling, Nick sank to his knees, holding a hand to the blood oozing from his cheek. The Colonel was about to lash him again when Sarah made a snap decision. The situation was about to go totally out of control; some of the soldiers had drawn their rifles. In a moment Callahan could be dead. She stepped between the two men, and facing Callahan began screaming at him. Part of her rage was real—the bastard had deceived her and put her own position in jeopardy—but part was for the benefit of Colonel Gau, and it had to work. She was depending on her acting ability to pull them through.

"You son of a bitch! You lied to me! You lied to the UN! You lied to everybody, you bastard!" She sensed that she had the Colonel's full attention. He had lowered his car antenna and was regarding her intently, a shade of surprise wrinkling his features. "Do you have any idea how many people you've screwed on this?" she continued to scream. "Do you even give a damn?"

Taking a deep breath—telling herself: *Okay, Sarah, go for it*—she smacked Callahan across the face with her open palm. She struck with all of her force, holding back nothing. With a cry he fell from his knees flat out on the ground.

Colonel Gau watched the scene unfold with a strange glint in his eyes. After a moment a slight grin creased his habitual impassivity. Sarah was certain she was reading his expression correctly: He was fascinated by Nick's loss of face to her, a mere woman. She was sure of it. Some of the soldiers were also laughing, reinforcing his humiliation. Humiliation may be the only thing that would save him. As he lay sprawled on the ground, she spit on him. She then turned to the Colonel, breathless, wide-eyed; she was determined to touch his ego and massage it. She was certain that was their one and only chance.

"Colonel Gau," she began, her manner both fearful and penitent. "You are a man of honor, and this man is a fool. A stupid fool . . ." She did not engage his eyes but kept hers lowered in the subordinate position. "Just look at him, Colonel. What kind of a man is he? Do you think such a little man would dare cross you again? He tries to trick a woman and he fails. He is a worm."

The Colonel could not resist a tiny, vain smile. Sarah, seeing this with the briefest of glances, pressed her advantage. "As a man of honor," she said, almost in a whisper, "I plead with you to show mercy. . . ."

Colonel Gau cast a cool glance at Callahan, still sprawled out and holding a hand to his wound. He slowly turned back to Sarah, and she could not read his expression. Her life and Callahan's depended on this moment.

She said, "Not mercy for him, Colonel. I'm not asking for that. The man deserves no mercy. But for the people he serves—your people. I am asking for them. Think of how many will die if he's not there to help them. Think of how many will thank you if you show mercy for their sake."

She sensed that the man was weakening. A softer, more reflective light suddenly suffused his eyes. She pressed her advantage, saying, "You save this man and the name of Colonel Gau will be remembered. You will be a hero to the people. . . ."

His eyes fixed on her, he said finally, "You can proceed. But first we examine all crates. You take only medicine and food supplies." He turned toward Callahan, who was slowly rising to his feet, and spit. "Vermin," he said. "Traitor." He took a step toward Callahan when Sarah said soothingly, "You see how frightened he is of you? You are a great and powerful man, Colonel. By saving his life, you save the lives of thousands of people."

13

Two hours later the trucks lumbered through the roadblock, leaving Colonel Gau and his soldiers behind. Sarah, squeezed against Callahan now as Tao drove, stared straight ahead, too furious to speak. Callahan held a rag to his cheek. He glanced at Tao but the Cambodian's eyes were locked on the road ahead. Tao had decided that these two crazy white people would have to fight it out between themselves

Without warning, shocking Tao out of his thoughts, Sarah suddenly leaned over and wrenched on the handbrake. The truck lurched to a halt with a squeal of metal and a smell of burning rubber. She opened the door and jumped out.

"Jesus," Callahan said.

Tao pounded on the steering wheel. "Crazy woman. Nothing but trouble, boss."

Callahan caught up with her a few paces down the jungle road. They walked stride for stride in silence.

"You've got to get back in the truck," Callahan said finally. "We've got a lot of ground to cover. It's better that we do it in daylight."

She stared straight ahead as she said, "You are amazing, you know that? I save your worthless life, I beg and plead for you, and not so much as a thank you. Not a speck of gratitude. Nothing."

Callahan gave a small shrug. "Thank you."

She stopped and turned to him. Her face was red and blotched with emotion. "What is it with you and suffering? Do you do this for kicks? Nick Callahan suffers for all our sins. Jesus!" She punched his shoulder—not gently. "I trusted you."

"Things have changed," Callahan muttered. "We do what we have to do. Sometimes you play games with the bad guys. That's the way it is. Anyway, you knew why you were coming—you knew the deal."

"Don't you dare tell me what I know and don't know," she snapped. "Don't you *dare* presume to know why I came. You use my contacts, you get Elliot to beg for you, and then when you get me here you fuck me over for a gunrunner. You put my work and the UN in jeopardy."

Callahan stared at her, absorbing her anger. When he spoke his voice was low, devoid of emotion. It was as though he was measuring each word to make sure that he was getting it right.

"I came here to help these people. The only way I can get medicine to them is to transport guns and technical support. That's what it's come down to. It stinks. I know that. It sickens me. But what do you want me to do? Watch some kid die of measles because I won't bend the rules? Is that a price worth paying? Or am I killing more than I save? You seriously believe I don't worry about that? That I don't think about it every minute of every day?" He grabbed Sarah's arm and pulled her close, staring deep into her eyes. "What's worse? You tell me that. You tell me what I should do."

The refugee village located deep in the Cambodian jungle was a junkyard on stilts. As the trucks pulled up, Sarah could glimpse through doorways women and children, some on crutches, others just crippled from disease and years of malnutrition, still others missing limbs. She tried to compare the scene to her first exposure to Ethiopia, and she felt that Africa was probably worse. But then she wondered if she had just become hardened to suffering. Certainly she was light-years removed from that naïve girl who had first set foot on African soil, having no idea what to expect and believing that goodness could cure the ills of the world. Now she was not so sure about happy endings. She was still shocked and hurt that Callahan had tried to smuggle in guns—and perhaps more hurt that he wasn't willing to confide in her. But even that shock was beginning to wear off. "We do what we have to do," he had told her. And who was she, with her sheltered life and many privileges, to say that he wasn't right? Once again, as had happened years earlier, only this time with more force, she wondered if she was living in the real world.

She stepped down from the truck and walked behind Callahan to the hospital, a raised platform under corrugated sheets—even cruder, she thought, than the setup in Ethiopia. Ailing refugees stood outside of huts hardly more substantial than cardboard boxes, staring at her as though she were an apparition. Poverty and neglect were everywhere; the very air, humid and barely breathable, smelled of defeat.

When Joss and Kat rushed to greet her, her heart lifted.

"Sarah," Kat cried, "just look at you. You look great!"

"Hello, Kat. Hi, Joss. Well, I'm back. You just can't get rid of me."

"You must be a damn fool, is all I can say," Joss said with a wide grin. "Some people never learn—yours truly at the head of the list."

"I was surprised to hear you were coming," Kat said. "I thought you'd gone respectable on us."

"Apparently not. I guess Joss has me pegged."

She was aware of Callahan standing off to one side, saying nothing. When she glanced at him he looked quickly away and started a discussion with a local nurse, dressed in white, at the entrance to the hospital.

When Elliot Hauser appeared, she gave him a hug and whispered in his ear, "I didn't know Buddha does gunrunning. That comes as a great surprise."

She smiled teasingly, but he looked embarrassed and did not return her smile.

"I'm sorry," he said. "A lot has happened in the last five years. A lot of changes. We'll talk about it later."

"You could've told me in London. I had a right to be let in on things."

"You're right, Sarah. But then you probably would have turned us down. I couldn't take that chance. We're desperate."

"So trust is no longer part of the equation."

"We'll have to work on that," he said, attempting a smile. "I guess there's repair work to do."

She nodded. "I think so, Elliot."

Kat, impatient to break into their discussion, dug an elbow into Joss's ribs and said to Sarah, "Hey, I've got some big news. You know I married this lug? Can you believe it? I must've been out of my mind."

"Love at first sight," Joss said with a dry smile. "Only took us seven years."

Sarah kissed their cheeks and said, "Congratulations, Joss. And to you, my dear, good luck. I hope you can keep him in line."

"I'm working on it."

Callahan came up, shaking his head. "No guns," he said to Elliot. "Confiscated by Gau."

Elliot looked at him sharply. "That's bad news."

"I've got worse. It wasn't the guns that got to Gau. It was the intelligence files."

"What intelligence files? What are you talking about?"

"Steiger fucked us, but good. Stuff like that—secret government documents—it can get you killed. It almost got me killed." He flashed a quick glance at Sarah.

"Steiger never mentioned any files," Elliot said. "That wasn't part of the deal."

"Well, he's hardly going to warn us in advance, is he? 'Oh by the way, boys, I'm going to fuck you over. Hope you don't mind.'"

"You know this changes everything," Elliot said.

"Bullocks. I don't buy that at all."

"Nick—"

"Come on, man. We've got to vaccinate and then get the hell out of here. I'm not wasting it."

"There isn't time. The KR troops were down yesterday looking for you. We have to go. I can see us caught in a crossfire between the Viets and the

KR, and if that happens we're dead along with the refugees."

Callahan shook his head, his eyes blazing. "Not until we've vaccinated these people."

"Nick—sorry. But you are *not* risking our lives for this."

"You want me to tell the children that? Do you, El? Is that what you want?"

The two old friends stood eyeball to eyeball in the grip of a furious silence, neither willing to back off. Callahan broke the silence, saying, "We vaccinate first. That's the way it has to be. We didn't come all the way here to run out when things go wrong."

At daybreak, Callahan, Kat, and Monica were rapidly vaccinating the young children, while Elliot, Joss, and Sarah, with a number of local helpers, were organizing for a quick withdrawal, packing the trucks to the gunwales with everything transportable. There was an occasional murmured command or a request, but for the most part they worked in silence, efficiently and quickly. They were aware of the danger they were facing and that every moment counted.

Callahan, examining a young patient, said, "Monica, bring me the IV sacs."

There was no reply. Callahan looked up in irritation. "Monica, the IV sacs. On the double, girl."

Monica stood absolutely still. Following her

frightened gaze, Callahan saw the Khmer Rouge commander, Ma Sok, standing at the doorway. He was a small, scarred stick of a man, the color of cherry wood. He was holding a pistol and carrying a machete in his belt. On either side of him were guerrillas in sandals and scarves, all armed. The room fell silent. Kat, quickly looking away, continued quietly to vaccinate. Some of the more inquisitive refugees pushed in close to witness whatever was about to happen.

"Stand back," Ma Sok shouted. Everyone froze.

Ma Sok stepped forward, facing Hauser. Like Kat, Callahan continued to vaccinate. The soldiers fanned out and covered the room with raised rifles. Ma Sok began to yell at Elliot, waving his arms, spit spraying from his lips.

"He says we're thieves," Elliot said quietly. "He says we stole a shipment of guns and sold them to the Viets. And the files—he wants the files. We're going to have to pay."

Callahan looked up as he removed a needle from the tiny upper arm of a young girl. "Tell him we're saving his bloody people. Tell him the shipment was taken from us at gunpoint." He turned to Tao, who was standing unobtrusively against a back wall. "Tao, explain it to the commander."

Both Elliot and Tao bantered back and forth with Ma Sok in Cambodian. As the commander's voice rose and his movements became more agitated, it was clear to Callahan they weren't getting through to him.

Tao broke off, turning to Callahan. "He say he don't give a shit about the people. He want the delivery he was promised. The files most of all."

"He's threatening us, Nick," Elliot added. "This doesn't look good."

"So tell him whatever he wants to hear," Callahan said without looking up. "Just buy us some time."

Elliot and Tao translated, talking over each other in their nervousness.

Ma Sok grunted out his reply.

"He wants us to . . ." Elliot turned to Tao. "I didn't get that last part."

"He wants us to what?" Callahan said impatiently.

Ma Sok screamed something else, glaring hard at Callahan.

"Pailin," Tao said to Elliot, taking a step away from the commander's anger.

Elliot, his voice suddenly shaky, said, "He wants us to make amends now. He insists we go with him to Pailin. You know what that means . . . we go there, we're not coming back."

"We die," Tao said in a whisper. "They torture us."

Ma Sok screamed once more, shaking his fist.

Glancing fearfully at Callahan, Tao said, "He say *now.*"

Callahan put down his syringe for a moment. Sarah, who along with Joss had rushed up to the hospital, the trucks loaded and ready to roll, thought he was the calmest person in the room, along with Kat and Monica. At least they had a job to do.

Callahan said, "Tell the commander that Sarah's from the UN. Tell him the UN is very important to big god Angka. And if anything— anything at all—happens to her or us, the UN's going to crucify him."

Tao swiftly translated, with a series of swooping gestures and half bows. Ma Sok listened impassively, never blinking.

Sarah produced her ID and tried to hand it to Ma Sok, but he waved it away. He continued to glare at Callahan. Then suddenly he began to scream again.

"What's he yelling, Elliot?"

"I'm missing most of it. He's talking so fast and there's a lot of idiom."

"He say you CIA agent working for Vietnam," Tao said. "One of us must die. He need to take a life."

Ma Sok continued to scream, continuing to spray volumes of spit. Callahan wiped his face and screamed back at him. "Why don't you shut the fuck up?" He started to rise from the bench, his fists clenched.

"No, Nick, no, man," Elliot said. "Do nothing. Don't provoke him."

Ma Sok, challenged by the violence in Callahan, raised his pistol. A kind of rictus distorted his features; it may have been a smile. When he spoke his voice was low and harsh.

"English doctor," Tao translated, "you say all you care about is my people."

"Tell him that's my job," Callahan snapped. "That's the only reason I'm here."

"He say you not belong here," Tao translated again.

Ma Sok's eyes shifted. A baby lay peacefully on a blanket at the end of the long bench, waiting to be inoculated. His mother stood beside him. She ran a hand over the child's silky black hair. Ma Sok barked a command to a woman guerrilla, who removed a grenade from her belt and slipped it into the baby's lap, then retreated quickly along with everyone standing near except for the baby's mother who began to scream, a hand to her mouth. As she continued to scream she started to advance on Ma Sok. He calmly raised his rifle and shot her in the face. She fell to the floor, blood streaming from a gaping hole in her cheek. He spoke quietly to the hushed room, his voice measured and dark.

"To Angka," Tao translated shakily. "He say life mean nothing. We serve only Angka. Now you will see."

The baby, unaware that his mother was no longer beside him, considered his new toy. He rolled the grenade across his stomach, then curled his fingers into the ring. The baby's mother—still alive—uttered a strangled low shriek as she tried to crawl toward him. He was now totally absorbed in this fascinating metal toy. He tugged on the pin with both hands as he gurgled contentedly to himself.

Callahan was standing now, poised in a slight crouch, his eyes fixed on Ma Sok.

"For God's sake," Kat cried out. "He's just a baby."

Ma Sok whirled toward her on the heel of his left boot, screaming at her in Cambodian. He leaped forward, withdrew his machete and swiped it across her cheek. Moaning, Kat staggered back; she clutched her bleeding face. Joss and Sarah rushed toward her, and as Ma Sok drew his machete back and began to advance on Joss, Callahan suddenly launched himself at the commander. They collided and tumbled together to the floor, legs flying, trading punches. The KR guerrillas, uncertain what to do, instinctively reached for their weapons, but no one fired. After a fierce struggle, Callahan managed to wrest the machete from the much smaller man's grasp. He slammed it with all of his strength against Ma Sok's throat; Ma Sok gave a strangled cry. Eyeing the guerrillas closely, Callahan swiveled Ma Sok around as a protective shield.

"Nick," Elliot implored as he moved toward Callahan. "This isn't going to work."

"Tell them to drop their fucking weapons," Callahan roared. *"I mean now.* Otherwise I'll kill this son of a bitch. Tell them, Tao."

"Stop!" Ma Sok screamed at his troops in Cambodian. "Do nothing."

"Let him go," Elliot told Callahan. "We're outnumbered. We can't win this. . . ."

Utterly focused, Callahan pushed the machete more firmly against Ma Sok's throat as the commander continued to scream orders at his troops. The soldiers were confused and in disarray: some kept their rifles at the ready, others lowered them.

"No—*no,*" Sarah screamed as the baby managed to pull the pin free of the grenade.

"Oh my God!" Elliot said, and reached toward the baby.

"Elliot," Callahan shouted, *"Don't . . . no!"*

He broke away from Ma Sok to move after Elliot, who had swiped the grenade free of the baby's hands. He rushed to the window, which was partially open, and hurled it out. Elliot then stooped to pick up the baby, now purple in the face and howling with frustration. "There, there," he said, a pacifying smile on his face.

Ma Sok screamed an order and the woman guerrilla raised her rifle and squeezed out a round. Without a sound Elliot toppled forward, and even as he fell he twisted his body to avoid landing on the crying child.

An instant later the grenade exploded just outside the window. Enraged refugees were now storming the hospital room, wielding machetes, rocks, wire hangers—anything at hand. In the midst of the confusion, Joss grabbed a gun from the floor and emptied the chamber into Ma Sok. Seeing their fallen leader, the guerrillas fled.

Sarah knelt over Elliot, holding his lifeless body in her arms. "You bastards," she wailed. "You bastards. You bastards . . ."

Callahan stood beside her, too shocked to move, to react to his friend's death. The baby, now over its tantrum, was pawing at Elliot's face and gurgling softly.

"We have to leave here," Callahan said softly. "They'll be back. I know these people. They will have to avenge Ma Sok's death." He spoke to Sarah, not once looking at Elliot's body. "There's a good chance we'll all be dead by the end of the day."

The Khmer Rouge soldiers had the last word. Before retreating from the compound they dropped hand grenades on the three trucks, reducing them to useless piles of jagged metal. The only option now was to walk to safety. Beneath a canopy of jungle growth, which turned brilliantly sunny days into extended periods of darkness, Callahan led a ragged column of three hundred refugees as they inched their way through the humid undergrowth. Joss walked beside him, his mood sullen and dark. Tao and Sarah followed a few strides behind them. Kat and the medical assistants helped the more ailing and infirm. Everyone stumbled over hidden roots that matted the jungle floor, struggling for each step.

Strangely, there were few complaints; it was as though they knew they had this one chance to live and this one only; it was as though the violence that resulted in the death of Elliot Hauser, beloved by the refugees, had sent mortal tremors through everyone. It was now or never.

The snakelike procession forged on through the afternoon, despite the precarious condition of most of the refugees. They possessed an iron resolve to survive. They were on the move and each step was one less step they would have to take and one more step toward safety. With Elliot gone, they put their faith in the doctor. He had shown his true strength by standing up to the evil commander. He was not a kind man like Elliot Hauser, he did not speak their language, but he had shown his true courage and they respected him for that and would follow him wherever he led.

At one of their brief stops, Callahan squatted beside the path, a military map spread out on the ground. He, Joss, and Tao studied it, Callahan working with a compass. His finger traced a wavy blue line on the map. He said, "As long as we hold due east, we should hit the river."

"That's about two miles," Joss said, shaking his head.

"The camp's another three miles north," Callahan said. "There"—he pointed with a finger—"just over the Thai border."

Joss gestured with his thumb at the refugees sprawled out on the ground. "Jesus, mate, how are these poor bastards going to walk that far? You might as well ask them to walk to bloody London."

They heard a crack of gunfire off in the distance, to the west. They listened intently.

"KR," Tao said.

"Yeah," Callahan said. "They've reached the compound. At this rate they'll catch up to us."

"Well, we'd better get a move on then," Joss said.

An hour later, the weather had changed. Accompanied by loud cracks of thunder rain was pouring down on them. The ground steamed with humidity. Tao had explained to the refugees that KR troops were closing in on them and they could not afford any more rest stops. They understood and did not complain: Either they reached the Thai border ahead of the KR or they would all die. There was no other option. So they trudged on through the downpour, hungry and exhausted, some of them delirious with disease, but not a single refugee was left behind. They slipped and slid down a riverbank and began forging the river. An old man had fainted just as they reached the river. Joss lifted him onto his shoulders.

Callahan stood at the river's edge, motioning people across. When the stretcher carrying Elliot Hauser's body passed by, carried by two male medical helpers, he looked away and for an instant closed his eyes.

"Come on," he shouted. "Nearly there. Let's go! Go!"

Tao translated his words to the refugees.

The sound of gunfire was louder now, their pursuers drawing closer. Callahan pulled out a radio from his canvas knapsack. "Sierra Tango," he said. "Six-one-nine. This is outpost Red Seven. . . ."

There was no reply.

The line was advancing more slowly now. Even the approaching gunfire and the prospect of torture and certain death could not propel them ahead any faster. They were at the limit of their endurance. Callahan moved along the line until he reached Sarah. She was staggering forward holding two small children in her arms. Her face was white with strain as she struggled against her own physical limits. Callahan took one of the children from her.

"You okay?" he said.

"Fine."

As he clutched the child to his chest he gave the radio another try.

"Sierra Tango . . . Sierra Tango . . . Six-one-nine. Come in. . . ." He shook his head. "Shit!"

At that moment he noticed Tao running along the line calling out to him. "Boss! Boss! Listen. . . ."

The whopping of helicopter blades was suddenly audible and growing louder. Callahan squinted up through the dripping jungle canopy and spotted two helicopters sweep by barely above the tree line.

"Vietnamese," he said.

In the near distance they could hear rockets starting to go off. The firefight was very near.

"Let's keep pushing," Callahan said. "We've bought some time." He started yelling for the refugees to pick up the pace in the few broken phrases of Cambodian he had learned.

As they trudged ahead in silence a gloom as palpable as the steady rain descended on Callahan. *I bring death with me wherever I go. My mission is to save lives, and yet I was responsible for JoJo and I lost him. Today I lost Elliot, my best friend. If I'd handled Ma Sok differently Elliot might still be alive. We might not have had to make this march. Who's next—Sarah? Am I going to kill her too out of the best possible motives? Dr. Nick, the great white doctor. Nick . . . the angel of death.*

The rain suddenly picked up in intensity. At the front of the line, Joss and Kat were urging the exhausted refugees forward. Joss had been aware for some minutes that the old man he carried was no longer breathing; the gravity of his body was increasingly pulling Joss down. Dead weight, he thought. He lowered the old man's warm corpse to the ground and pulled his ragged shirt up over his face. A concussive detonation caused Joss to look up sharply; land mines were exploding in the jungle ahead of them; they seemed to be exploding everywhere. Joss stared in amazement. Callahan and Sarah joined Joss and Kat as they stared ahead, listening, straining to see through the jungle darkness.

"It's the rain," Callahan said finally, shaking his head in disbelief. "Can you believe it? It's coming down so hard it's triggering the mines."

When the smoke from the explosions began to clear they could see in the distance, barely visible, a UNHCR encampment. Through binoculars Joss made out a series of small fires, a helicopter pad, and two women carrying water buckets. He turned to Callahan and grinned. "Looks like salvation, mate."

Callahan nodded. He was too full of grief and exhaustion to fully appreciate their achievement or to feel any sense of relief.

"Good," he said quietly, from some deep space within himself. He turned to Sarah. "We made it."

"Yes, Nick. We made it."

The funeral for Elliot was held late the following day, after Callahan's group and all the refugees had settled into the UNHCR camp. About twenty mourners were gathered around a makeshift funeral pyre. Elliot's corpse was elaborately shrouded and a refugee woman bathed his face with scented water. A tiny clang of bells sounded rhythmically. Huge clouds presaged the coming of a monsoon, and the heavy air was barely breathable.

"I wasn't sure where to build it," Joss whispered as though in church, checking Callahan for his approval. "I know he went on about the East and souls and stuff. But, I don't know—somehow I figured he'd want to be facing West. Looking toward home."

Joss awaited a nod from Callahan, some sign that he had done the right thing, but the man seemed lost in thought. He had either not heard or refused to respond.

"Well," Joss said through the silence, "someone want to say something?"

"Only that he had a gentle soul," Sarah said through her tears. "He was the kindest human being I've ever known. God . . ." She faltered, then continued, saying, "God must be delighted to have him back."

Everyone else was too grief-stricken to speak.

Joss stared at the pyre and said, "Sarah got it right. Elliot was one sweet and righteous gentleman. So sail on, mate. Sail on. . . ."

And that was it. There was nothing else to be said, or no words adequate to the occasion. Sarah stepped up to the pyre and from her pocket she removed the knot of eternity that Elliot had given her five years earlier and which she carried with her everywhere. She looped it around one of the twigs beside the fire, placed it on Elliot's chest and then stepped back.

Callahan stared at the knot of eternity and then slowly looked away. It was impossible to read his expression.

The wind was building steadily and two women refugees struggled to keep the fire going. Joss cast a worried look at the sky.

"You're facing a losing battle there, ladies," he said in his special mixture of English and Cambodian. "It's going to piss a Dublin pint any minute."

Kat, crying silently, gave him a rough shove. "Do you always have to be so practical, you oaf?"

Callahan studied the fire without blinking, as though in a trance, as the rain slowly put it out.

Sarah stared at him, trying to will him out of his misery. "Say something," she whispered. "Tell him how you felt about him."

He turned to her, face flushed, his eyes blazing. "He's gone. He can't hear anything, don't you understand that?" Without another word he stormed away.

That evening, Callahan was sitting on his bed in the Red Cross station, dead still, his head in his hands. Sarah entered quietly and stared at him.

"Nick?" she said.

He gave no response. She put out a hand to touch his shoulder and he shrank away.

"Don't," he said, his face clenched with tension.

She quickly pulled her hand away. "Nick," she said again.

"I don't want to talk about it," he said, still not looking up.

"It wasn't your fault. You mustn't blame yourself."

He finally looked at her, and the pain she saw in his eyes made her catch her breath. "Yes it was. If I'd listened to Elliot, none of this would've happened. And I couldn't even bury him properly. He died because of me and I couldn't even give him a decent fucking burial. What kind of a man does that make me?"

"Elliot wanted to dedicate his life to helping others," she said. "And in the end he died for them. You should be proud of him. Miss him, Nick—but be proud of him."

There was a long silence as they stared at each other, reaching out, trying to connect and to bridge the terrible gulf of Elliot's passing.

"I don't know what I'm going to do without him." He spoke almost in a whisper.

Sarah stared at him, feeling helpless. Was there any way to reach this emotionally drowning man?

"I can't stop now," he said, his head down. "I've got to keep going. There's so much—there's still so much to do."

He looked so utterly drained. She wanted to reach out and comfort him, but she knew him well enough to know that he had to deal with his grief his way, on his own terms.

"I worry about you being here," she said. "I'm scared of what might happen to you." She waited for his response, but there was none. He continued to stare at the floor. She moved a step closer to him. "Five years, Nick. Five years of waking up every morning and wondering if you're okay, where you are, if you're still alive." She swallowed and said softly, "I love you so much."

He rose slowly from the bed and moved toward her and her arms welcomed him. They kissed, and then he pulled back and gazed into her eyes.

"Five years," he said. He shook his head. "I know. . . ."

He kissed her again and the kiss turned into a long embrace. They were locked together pouring love into each other. Holding onto each other, they walked lockstep to the bed, Callahan's arms clasped around Sarah's waist. They fell onto the bed, and Callahan said, "Five years waiting for this moment. . . ."

Later, they lay next to each other on the bed, holding hands. Happy, relaxed.

"Shall I ring for room service," Callahan said, grinning.

"A little air-conditioning would be lovely," she said. "And a piece of chocolate cake."

"I can provide the air-conditioning," he said,

and blew in her face. She pulled back, laughing. They lay for a moment in silence, in the easy stillness of a new kind of intimacy.

"How did you meet Henry?" Callahan said finally.

"Staring at a Rothko."

He turned and gave her a deadpan look. "What's that? Some kind of dishwasher?"

"The painter."

"Ah."

"As though you didn't know. I worked in a gallery. And one day Henry came in."

"How old were you?"

"Way too young."

"But you stayed together."

"It was over long ago. We both know that." She hesitated. "We stayed together for Jimmy."

"You love him very much, don't you?"

Sarah nodded, and for a moment her smile was faraway, in another place. "The best and the brightest, my Jimmy," she said.

They kissed, then Callahan turned quickly away. He rose from the bed and began to dress. His expression was troubled. "You know, I need to start making plans to go to New York. I have to see Elliot's parents and tell them what happened."

"How long will you be away?"

"I don't know," he said, avoiding her eyes. "No idea . . ."

She reached out and touched his arm. "Nick—

what is this? One minute you're so loving and then this coldness, this distance. What are you doing? I don't understand. . . ."

He turned on her suddenly, his voice constricted with emotion. "I'm absolutely crazy about you, Sarah. I can't stop thinking about you. You're always in my mind, you're in my heart, you're in every fucking beat of me. But I can't go there with you. I can't do it. Look what happens to people around me. I'm not good for you."

"That's not true!"

"No, listen to me. Believe me, if I could live this life again I'd never leave you for a second. But you belong with your family and I belong here, and there's nothing I can do about it, because whichever way I look at it, somebody always gets hurt."

He hung in the doorway about to leave, when he suddenly lunged forward for one last passionate kiss.

"Sarah . . ."

And then he was gone. Sarah stared at the doorway, now empty of the man she loved. Tears filled her eyes.

PART

3